D0059750

One by Sea

WEEKLY READER
CHILDREN'S BOOK CLUB

Weekly Reader Children's Book Club

presents

ONE BY SEA

by Scott Corbett

Illustrated by Victor Mays

An Atlantic Monthly Press Book
LITTLE, BROWN and COMPANY
Boston · Toronto

COPYRIGHT © 1965 BY SCOTT CORBETT

ALL RIGHTS RESERVED. NO PART OF THIS BOOK MAY BE REPRODUCED
IN ANY FORM OR BY ANY ELECTRONIC OR MECHANICAL MEANS IN-
CLUDING INFORMATION STORAGE AND RETRIEVAL SYSTEMS WITHOUT
PERMISSION IN WRITING FROM THE PUBLISHER, EXCEPT BY A REVIEWER
WHO MAY QUOTE BRIEF PASSAGES IN A REVIEW.

LIBRARY OF CONGRESS CATALOG CARD NO. 65-10583

WEEKLY READER CHILDREN'S BOOK CLUB EDITION. SENIOR DIVISION.

ATLANTIC–LITTLE, BROWN BOOKS
ARE PUBLISHED BY
LITTLE, BROWN AND COMPANY
IN ASSOCIATION WITH
THE ATLANTIC MONTHLY PRESS

Published simultaneously in Canada
by Little, Brown & Company (Canada) Limited

PRINTED IN THE UNITED STATES OF AMERICA

To Jacob Whitford

A good friend and
leader of boys

One by Sea

One

IF HE COULD help it, Nye Gorham never walked straight home to his grandfather's great Georgian house after school. He always went roundabout by way of the waterfront. There he dawdled along past the slips and wharves to see what new ships had appeared in the harbor of the busy English Channel port.

"Please, sir, is there any new ship in from America?" he would ask any seaman or longshoreman or clerk who looked half inclined to tolerate a question from a schoolboy. The answers would vary.

"America, lad? Not today."

Or something that sounded like "Nowt!" which apparently meant "No" or "Not" or "Nought," he was never sure which.

Or perhaps some good-natured old sea-dog who had seen him before would lay a horny hand on his shoulder and march him to the edge of a wharf and point:

"See that bark next the *Devon Maid*, her with her mains'l yards dropped? She's the *Carrollton*, twenty-seven days out of Baltimore."

"Not Boston?" Nye would say, disappointed. Any American ship might bring a letter or some message from his father, but Boston was home and a Boston vessel most likely to do so.

Or perhaps some ancient peg-leg who had reason to remember 1812 would growl, "Yankee scum!" and spit none too tidily, and Nye would make a face at him, patriotically, and run on before he had his ears boxed. Nye had been born an American, in Boston, and his mother's English blood did not change that to his way of thinking. Much as he had loved her, much as he missed her, and much as he respected his stern British grandsire, he was not proving manageable on this point. His grandfather — no mean antagonist, with his bristling muttonchop whiskers and hard blue eyes — insisted on considering him an English boy who was half American. Nye no less sturdily insisted on considering himself an American boy who was half English. Grandfather Kendrick was a good man, but a man with a passion for arranging other people's lives.

"There's the question of an education, my boy, and that you can best obtain right here where you are," he was fond of pointing out to Nye. "A good solid British

4

schooling," he would say complacently, with his back to the fire and the skirt of his frock coat hoisted to expose his good solid British backside to the warmth. "Even your father can hardly fail to agree that that's the thing for you, now that you're here and doing well."

"But . . . but I'd like to go home, Grandfather. I'd like to see my father."

"Home! What sort of home would you go to, with a father who would never be in it, always off to sea? When do you think you'd see him? And who'd look after you, who'd see to it you got a proper education, boy?"

"Well, my Uncle Daniel . . ."

"Stuff and nonsense, lad! We don't even know that your uncle wants you. No, the place for you is here, with the proper sort of schoolmasters in the proper sort of school."

And Nye would listen with a lonely, trapped feeling, all but overwhelmed by the odds against him. With each day that passed, America and home seemed farther and farther away.

It was a fine September afternoon, with a brisk on-shore breeze to put a whiff of salt in the air. The sight of the harbor sparkling under slanting sunrays gave his heart a lift as Nye ran down Commerical Road toward the waterfront.

He ran with a light foot despite a certain stiffness caused by the caning he had received at school from the headmaster, Dr. Rixby. Well, he had deserved it, he supposed, because he had been warned again and again not to use what Dr. Rixby called "barbaric American expressions." The words had simply slipped out as he struggled with a Latin sentence — "What in tarnation does that mean?" he had muttered.

"I'll not have my school contaminated by Yankee barbarisms!" the good doctor had roared as he applied the birch with a degree of enthusiasm that made Nye bite hard to keep from crying out. Dr. Rixby had some justice on his side. At first the other boys had mocked Nye's expressions, but later they had taken to using them. As a guardian of the purity of the English tongue, the headmaster felt quite justified in beating Nye. Indeed, he sometimes seemed determined to beat the Yankee out of Nye if he could.

Slowing down for a moment to rub the tender spot, Nye gazed out over the harbor, and his eyes widened. Out in the roadstead, swinging gently with the tide, lay a ship that was unmistakably American. The rake of her sheer, the pitch of her masts — he had looked hard at enough ships by now to know.

6

There were also men along the docks now whom he knew, some even by name. An old fellow they called Canty, who was hard at work nearby splicing a hawser, was one of them.

"I say, Canty! Isn't that an American ship out there?" cried Nye, darting over so fast that his scuffed and battered satchel of schoolbooks dragged his arm back as it tried to catch up with him.

"Eh?" Canty, sitting cross-legged at his work, cocked an eye up at the boy and then squinted where he pointed. "Oh, her. Aye, lad. Slipped in this morning early. And she's what you're forever jawing about, too. She's out of Boston."

"Boston! Hooray!" Nye tore off his cap and waved it in a wild high circle above his head while his feet danced a jig. "Maybe now —"

"Why all this ruction about Boston?"

Nye felt sure he had told him why before, as he had many another of his waterfront acquaintances, but Canty was said to be forgetful, and he was glad to tell him again.

"It's my father! I may hear from him, or — or —" Nye never quite let himself think that perhaps his father might even rescue him in person, because that was too much to hope for. Once in a while he let himself go in a daydream, and imagined his father appear-

7

ing, tall and resplendent in his best shore-going suit
and carrying a cane every bit as fine as Grandfather's
gold-headed one, with the afternoon sun at his back so
that dazzling golden rays seemed to surround him and
shoot away from him in all directions. But Nye never
let himself forget that this was only a daydream.

"Is your dad in Boston, then?" asked Canty.

"He's captain of the *Ellen Gorham*, out of Boston
to Hong Kong, due back this month."

"The *Ellen Gorham*, ye say? What sort of vessel be
she?"

"A medium clipper. Named for my mother."

Canty's marlinespike bit into the hawser, laying the
strands apart, and then he looked up again more keenly
at Nye.

"Gorham, is it? And ye be the grandson of Mr.
Kendrick the banker, bain't ye? And your poor ma is
the one . . ."

"Yes. She died five months ago."

"Five months! And your dad half the world away at
the time in the China Seas, knowing nought about it,
I'll vow. And the news a-waitin' for him in Boston —
a sad homecoming, that!" Canty waved a hand toward the American merchantman. "Well, there she be,
the *Griffin*, out of Boston, and I hope she brings you
some word from the poor man!"

9

After one last longing look at the ship Nye turned and set his course straight for his grandfather's house. Best to be there in case someone did bring a message. As he hurried along he tried to think of some means by which he could see the ship's skipper. Being from Boston, he would know Nye's father, and might be able to give some news of him even if his father had sent no messages. Nye was occupied with the problem when he turned between the ornate stone pillars, so well suited in their stern dignity to guard his grandfather's carriage drive, and walked toward the stately house.

A dusty four-wheeler with a red-faced, plug-hatted driver on the box stood in the drive. Nye's heart leaped hopefully. His grandfather had many visitors, but most of them came in their own traps or carriages. This one was obviously hired.

Nye took his customary path to a rear door and let himself in. Cook was busy in the kitchen and did not hear him enter. Usually he stopped to talk to the squat, plump little woman to learn what interesting eatables she might be inveigled into parting with if a hungry boy approached the subject in the right way. At the moment, however, curiosity and hope overshadowed appetite.

He slipped through the pantry and pushed through the swinging door into the dining room, where orderly rows of tall carved chairs surrounded a vast gleaming table. He crossed the room to the hall that led to the front rooms — the large parlor, the small parlor, the study.

In the hall he came to a sudden uneasy stop. He was halted in his tracks by the sound of his grandfather's stentorian voice angrily overwhelming the halting words of someone who seemed to be having a coughing fit. Even the closed doors of the study could not muffle the words that were being exchanged.

"But, sir, I have been commissioned" — cough! cough! cough! — "I have his letter authorizing" — cough! cough! cough! — "authorizing me to —"

"And I say, hang his letter, sir!" retorted Grandfather Kendrick. "Take the boy away from his schooling to knock about in heathen places on a Yankee merchantman — has he lost his senses?"

"He will undertake the boy's" — cough! cough! — "his books" — cough! cough! cough!

"He'll see to his education himself, will he? Tutor the boy himself, indeed! And is that any substitute for sound British schooling?" demanded Grandfather Kendrick scornfully.

"That, sir, is for him" — cough! cough! — "to decide. He has a prior claim —"

"I am aware of his prior claim, sir," responded Nye's

grandfather in icy tones. "I am aware of it, and under the proper conditions I should respect it, even though his decisions ran violently counter to my own wishes and beliefs. The proper conditions, I say, sir. But putting aside all other considerations, sir, I have a more immediate reason for refusing you. It is obvious that you are a very ill man. In my opinion you have all you can do to look after yourself, without attempting to make yourself responsible for another person."

This blunt judgment plainly affronted the visitor. Through another cruel bout of coughing he managed to gasp out a few resentful words.

"You presume to suggest that I am not —"

"I say nothing of your character, sir. I cast no aspersions on your character, which I am in no position to judge, having but now made your acquaintance. I am speaking of your physical condition only, sir. And I consider you physically no fit person to entrust the boy to. I refuse to send my grandson on a three-thousand-mile voyage on an American vessel in the care of a man who, if you will forgive me for saying so, does not seem fit to attempt such a voyage."

"How dare you, sir!" cried the stranger, but with a telltale break in his voice that showed with what ruthless accuracy Mr. Kendrick had bared his own fears. "My health . . . I have come on this voyage expressedly to . . . I have been greatly improved until I set foot on this accursed land of yours," he finished with almost an invalid's whine.

"I am sorry to be plain about this, Mr. Willet," said Grandfather Kendrick, "but the facts cannot be denied. I cannot turn the boy over to you. Let his father come for him himself, and I will of course surrender him."

"But his father cannot come! The *Ellen Gorham* must sail again next month — a special consignment from New York City, a fortune involved . . ."

"Then I am sorry. Perhaps when he returns from that voyage, some arrangement can be made, some more suitable arrangement for the boy's safe passage, suitably supervised. In the meantime . . . good day, sir!"

A new fit of coughing smothered any further protest the stranger may have been about to make, and Grandfather Kendrick's voice was courteous and urbane now as he said, "Really, sir! May I offer you something? A glass of port, perhaps? If I were you, Mr. Willet, I should concentrate my concern solely on myself!"

With a suddenness that made Nye jump, the study doors were flung open and the stranger came out. Noticing the boy standing transfixed in the hall, he paused for an instant and swung his burning eyes in Nye's direction.

The impact of that sunken-eyed stare Nye could never forget. What he saw was a pale and wasted face, the mouth covered by a handkerchief above which two enormous eyes seemed to glow, each in its own dark cavern. And when Mr. Willet took the handkerchief from his mouth, it was delicately spotted with red.

For a mere instant the stranger stared at him, and Nye stared back, yet in that instant each knew the other forever and a day. Then the man turned away, strode toward the tall double doors, and let himself out, slamming a door convulsively behind him.

Grandfather Kendrick had come out of the study to watch his guest leave. And now his eyes and Nye's met in their turn.

For once his grandfather did not put the worst possible construction on Nye's actions. He seemed to understand at once that Nye had not sneaked into the hall to listen, but had come there by accident. For a moment his old stern face worked, twisting and trembling in its frame of fierce eyebrows and bristling muttonchop whiskers, as he studied Nye's face and judged from the look of it how much he had heard, how much he had understood. When he spoke, his voice, though gruff and severe, had a catch in it that Nye had never heard before.

"I cannot possibly entrust you to a man like that. He is a dying man." His jaw set for a moment, and then with an effort he went on. "Your father is well, and sends you his fondest regards. We can hope that after his next voyage . . . But in the meantime . . ."

For a moment they looked at each other as enemies, but loving enemies. Grandfather Kendrick's tortured face was that of a man who had ruthlessly and cruelly defended something that was very dear to him. With a heart that was at once unbearably heavy and yet full of a kind of warmth that hurt, Nye understood at last that in his way his grandfather loved him. He lowered his head, suddenly afraid of tears.

"Yes, Grandfather," he said blindly, and went quickly up the broad staircase to his room.

Two

AGAIN AND AGAIN, until he fell at last into an uneasy sleep, Nye went over the words he had heard exchanged between the stranger and his grandfather. He could remember every word that had been said, and the story he was able to put together from them made him feel like a caged animal.

His father had returned to Boston. Now the *Ellen Gorham* was to sail with a special cargo worth a fortune, and his father wanted Nye with him. That was the only possible explanation for Grandfather Kendrick's words, "Take the boy away from his schooling to knock about in heathen places on a Yankee merchantman — has he lost his senses?"

Around the Horn to the China Seas with his father on his father's ship! Nye's heart leaped like a wave at the thought of it, and plunged like a ship in a trough at the thought of not being able to go. "He'll see to his education himself, will he? Tutor the boy himself, indeed! And is that any substitute for sound British schooling?" Grandfather Kendrick had asked scornfully, but Nye felt the scorn was unjustified. His father knew a lot about books. Nye was sure he could teach him everything he needed to know.

Dinner had been a gloomy, silent affair. Not one word more had Grandfather offered on the subject of Mr. Willet's visit. Obviously, as far as he was concerned, the subject was closed, even though not forgotten. And Nye could not muster sufficient courage to bring up the topic himself. Nor could he see where he could possibly benefit by doing so. His grandfather's mind was made up, and Grandfather Kendrick had not become the most important banker in town by being a man who was easily swayed from his decisions.

From the window in his room Nye could catch a glimpse of the sea. A newly risen full moon laid a ribbon of silver on the calm waters beyond silvery fields squared off by the dark lines of hedgerows, and the lighthouse beam had begun its steady swing, almost unnecessary on such a night. Nye sat at the window, thinking, longing, despairing, until his head began to nod, and then at last he flung himself down on his bed and dug his face hard into his pillow.

The hours he spent in school next day might have been the fringes of a dream, so little did they touch him. Even the cruel sting of his Latin master's ferrule on the palms of his hands failed to center his attention on the peculiarities of Latin verbs. Nye could think only about Mr. Willet and the American brig *Griffin*. He could think only of hurrying to the harbor after school to see if she was still there. How soon would she sail? Was she already gone? The mere thought made him want to cry out in pain.

"Gorham!" Mr. Snodgrass, his Latin master, had reached the end of his patience, and not without reason. Mr. Snodgrass, pacing back and forth before the class in his billowing black gown, was used to being listened to with attention. Hands behind his back, he now loosed a thunderbolt. "Gorham, you will remain after classes today and give me a hundred lines before you leave!"

The sentence fell like an axe on Nye's neck. A hundred lines of Vergil! Now he would never get to the harbor! Too late he realized that today of all days he should have been careful, should have made an extra effort to concentrate on his studies and stay out of trouble. When classes were over and the other boys had all scampered away and their happy shouts of freedom had tormented his ears, Nye sat under the frowning gaze of Mr. Snodgrass and began to copy his lines.

Conticuēre omnēs intentīque ōra tenēbant . . .

Ninety-nine more! And if they were not exactly right Mr. Snodgrass would have him do them again. Meanwhile the day would fade, the shadows would creep across the green lawn outside the ivy-framed windows, and he would not dare make the long side trip to the harbor. He looked yearningly but without hope at the open window. To vault through it would be easy, but old Snodgrass would immediately raise the hue and cry, and Nye would not get far, with a dozen or more of the older boys on a playing field not a stone's throw away.

"Snodgrass, I require you for a moment," said a resonant voice, while a long finger beckoned imperiously. Lounging behind his desk, turning through the pages of a book, Snodgrass looked up and beheld Dr. Rixby.

"Certainly, sir," he said, springing to his feet.

Nye had of course instantly risen beside his seat, too. Dr. Rixby noticed him, requested an explanation, and got it.

"Praise God, not another of his Yankee barbarisms,

at least," he remarked, beetling his brows at the offender.

"No, sir," said Nye meekly.

"I want you to be well along with those lines when I return," warned Mr. Snodgrass.

"Yes, sir."

The two black-gowned figures bustled out in a dark swirl, and Nye was left with his Vergil. He started to sit down again at his desk, but never quite made it. Yonder was the window, open and inviting, and it was now or never. It was no time to think of dreadful punishments to come. It was a time to think only of a vague but insistent urge, with a desperate resolve behind it. A resolve, to be sure, that Nye had not even fully admitted to himself as yet.

On legs that prickled as painfully as though they had been switched, Nye walked to the window and looked out. On the playing field a boisterous rugby scrimmage was in progress. Nye cast a wild glance over his shoulder, half expecting to see a wrathful Snodgrass stride into the room with hand outstretched, clawing for his collar. The next instant Nye had vaulted through the window and dropped onto the turf below among the bushes.

His heart stood still while he listened for someone to cry, "You there! What are you up to?" But no such cry came. On his hands and knees he picked his way beneath the bushes along the side of the building. Reaching its end, he darted across a walk to a line of bushes that would screen him from the boys on the playing field. Now he could run like a deer, because his cover curved down to the stone pillars and iron gates of the main entrance to the school grounds. The gates were open. He slipped through and continued to run,

run, run, until he was in the streets of the town and far enough from the school to be safe. He did not even notice the closed carriage that had been standing in the road fifty yards from the gates; he did not see it start up when he appeared.

Panting and spent, but still trotting a few steps out of every dozen in his impatience to reach the harbor, Nye hurried down Commerical Road. The waterfront opened up before him.

And there, out in the roadstead, lay the *Griffin*, with barges beside her taking off cargo.

For a long time Nye stayed on the wharves, staring at the ship, knowing what he wanted to do, but with no idea as to how he could possibly do it. While a team of huge drayhorses clomped past on the cobblestones, pulling a wagon loaded with great hogsheads of molasses, Nye crouched on a stringpiece, keeping a pointless vigil. If only she had moved in alongside a wharf to discharge her cargo, so that perhaps he could find Mr. Willet and talk to him! But there she lay, far out in the harbor, aloof and inaccessible.

In the end there was nothing to do but turn away with a heavy heart and trudge home to his grandfather's house. Now he would have to face whatever unpleasantness would inevitably await him there, as sooner or later it would — and probably sooner, if he knew Mr. Snodgrass and Dr. Rixby.

"Hi! Wait up there!"

The nasal voice belonged to a big, lanky, skulking boy with a straw-colored hank of hair that fell down over unfriendly eyes like the strands of a frayed hempen line. The boys were near the bend of a narrow lane. There was not much chance to escape if this was some town boy out to bully a schoolboy. Nye swung around, dropped his satchel, and put his back to a wall, ready to fight if he had to. The boy looked tempted, but spat in a lordly way and waved his hand.

"Never mind making fists, I'm not goin' ter punch yer face," he said with an accent that sounded familiar, but not British. "I've got a message ter give yer, that's all. If'n yer want to go ter America, be on India Wharf across from the Queen's Tar at midnight ternight, that's all."

Nye's chest felt ready to burst.

"*Tonight?*"

"That's what I said, didn't I?"

"She sails in the morning?"

"First breath o' wind, she does. Know where India Wharf is, don't yer?"

"Yes, and the Queen's Tar, too! Who told you to tell me?"

The boy sniffed contemptuously. "That's fer me to know and you to guess. India Wharf — Queen's Tar — midnight ternight, that's all."

And with that he turned on his heel — which was bare and extremely dirty — and strode away with his head cocked back disdainfully, as if he didn't think much of his errand.

Scarcely able to breathe, Nye picked up his satchel and walked on blindly, moving solely by instinct. An old lady with a market basket and a cooper's apprentice carrying a bundle of barrel staves both jostled him and scolded him for not watching where he was going. Stopping in the doorway of a draper's shop, his head spinning with questions, he tried to think matters through. What should he do? Should he go back to his grandfather's house at all? Yes, he had to go back. He couldn't dodge around the streets until midnight. If he didn't appear at home, his grandfather would turn out half the town to search for him, and he would be found.

There was nothing to do but go home — for the present. If only he had tended to his studies and stayed out of trouble! But there was no use in crying over spilt milk. Now only one thing mattered: escape, tonight. Somehow he would have to manage it.

One glance at the granite-like set of his grandfather's jaw, with the whiskers standing out from his jowls like scrubby bushes from a cliffside, was enough to tell Nye what Grandfather Kendrick had to say even before he said it.

"Dr. Rixby sent Mr. Snodgrass to call on me at the bank not an hour ago. I was utterly astounded to hear what you had done. What possible explanation do you have for your conduct?"

Nye hung his head.

"I . . . I . . ."

"Speak up, boy! Why did you do it?"

"I had to leave, sir."

"Why? Where did you go?"

Nye had to say something, and he was not good at lying.

"To the harbor, sir," he admitted.

"The harbor?" Grandfather Kendrick made a show of astonishment, but the way his eyes narrowed showed that he was not altogether surprised. "Why did you go there?"

"I only wanted to see the American ship, sir."

"The *Griffin?*"

"Yes, sir."

"And only *seeing* her was worth the punishments

you knew would be in store for you for such outrageous disobedience of your schoolmasters?"

"I don't know, sir. But I wanted to see her."

"Only *see* her? Is that all you wanted to do?" his grandfather persisted with furious disbelief. "Didn't you have some ridiculous notion in your head of trying to slip aboard her and stow away, if you found she had moved in where you could get at her? Isn't that why you ran off down to the harbor?"

"No, sir," said Nye truthfully. He had thought of this course of action, to be sure, but had put it aside as being stupid, even if it had been possible. His grandfather would have known exactly where to look for him. He would have been discovered long before the ship sailed. But then, slipping aboard had seemed an impossibility, anyway. How could he reach the ship as long as she lay at anchor far out in the harbor?

Grandfather Kendrick stopped pacing to plant himself in front of Nye and thunder down at him.

"I should like to believe you, because I should dislike to think any grandson of mine would attempt any scheme so harebrained and so certain of failure. There's not a man on the wharves of this town would dare row you out to her. A score of them would report it to me at once if any of those Yankee scoundrels had the audacity to let you set foot in their longboat. You are

staying here, sir, until such time as your father sets forth some better arrangement than he did on this occasion, and you had best make up your mind to it. And now you will go to your room, and tomorrow we shall decide what's to be done about your disgraceful performance at school."

Nye was only too glad to be dismissed. He was terrified lest his grandfather should somehow get wind of the secret he was trying to keep locked tight in his mind. Tonight, when the house was still . . . Early to bed and early to rise was one of Grandfather Kendrick's cherished guideposts to success — he was not averse to mentioning it, and had often done so to Nye. By ten o'clock, if all went well, the whole household would be fast asleep. With one small exception, that is.

Once in his room, Nye spent some time thinking about the few possessions he should put into a small drawstring bag he had, but dared not actually gather them together as yet. He supposed he would go without his supper that night as his first punishment, and tried to disregard how hungry he was. At his window he watched dusk settle over the fields and the distant sea, watched darkness creep under the trees.

His door opened. Cook came in carrying a tray. Cook herself, not Margaret, the maid. Savory odors drew Nye from the window, beaming with pleasure and surprise.

"Close that door. Quickly!" muttered Cook with a guilty air. Nye hurried to obey and rushed back to inspect with sparkling eyes the sturdy slice of roast beef and the piping hot boiled potatoes and slices of well-buttered bread that adorned the tray.

"Master said you were to have the barest bite to eat and go straight to bed," Cook announced severely.

"What a jolly meal! You were good to bring it yourself, Cook."

"I don't trust that Margaret," said Cook with a sniff. "Besides, I've brought you a bit more than you were supposed to have. Something more on the order of bread and water was what your grandpapa had in mind, so tuck into this and put it out of sight, if you don't want me to lose my place."

Nye went straight to work. In a trice all damaging evidence against Cook had disappeared. She watched approvingly as he mopped the last drop of gravy from his plate with the last morsel of bread and popped it into his mouth.

"No one could look at that plate and say for sure it had even had bread on it, let alone anything more," she declared. "That ought to leave you feeling better. Now off to bed!"

Nye smiled up at her gratefully and longed to say something special to this good woman, to at least say good-by. But of course that was the last thing he could do. She had been devoted to his mother as well, and had waited on her hand and foot during her brief, terrible last illness, and yet now he dared not even say good-by. Impulsively he reached out and touched her plump hand as she started to pick up the tray.

"Thank you, Cook," he said earnestly. "Thank you very much."

"Well, now!" The little dumpling of a woman looked almost flustered, but pleased. "You're a good boy, no matter what you've done," she declared with a defiant nod, picked up the tray, and quickstepped to the door. "Off to bed, now!" she repeated, with a sharp glance back at him, and closed the door behind her.

Fortified by the unexpected food, Nye felt the rush of renewed confidence a good meal can always provide. In his imagination he was already there, waiting on India Wharf across from the Queen's Tar. It would be easy. All he had to do now was pass the time until it was safe to slip out of the house, and to do nothing in the meantime that would arouse the slightest suspicion.

To begin with, then, he must obey his grandfather's orders. Quickly undressing and pulling on his nightshirt, he blew out his lamp and sat down on the window seat, ready to leap into bed at the first sound of a footstep in the hall. The moon had risen now, not quite as full as last night's but still extremely bright. Too bright, in fact, to suit a boy who hoped to sidle inconspicuously down through the streets of the town to the waterfront at an hour when young boys were not supposed to be abroad. By the time he left the house, however, few persons other than the watchmen would be in the streets. He would only have to keep a sharp eye out for the watchmen and stay clear of them, and all would be well.

Now he had only to wait.

Three

WAITING was the worst part of all. He stayed by the tall casement window for a long, long time, gazing out at the quiet fields. There was nothing he could do to pass the time, because he dared not make a sound or show a light. Once he stretched out on the bed and grew almost drowsy — and sprang up with horror as he realized he had nearly dropped off to sleep. The thought of waking to find it was morning and the *Griffin* had sailed without him was enough to make him pace the room in a frenzy of fear, shaking his head furiously to bring himself thoroughly awake. After an eternity a distant clock struck at last. The town clock. One . . . two . . . three . . .

Nine! Only nine o'clock after all this endless waiting! The thought of another hour of it seemed more than he could bear, and yet he knew it would be foolhardy to leave any sooner, before his grandfather had had a chance to get soundly to sleep.

Outside, at the end of the hall, the stairs creaked. Nye flew into bed, pulled the covers up around his neck, and settled himself on his side with his cheek crammed against his pillow. He forced himself to breathe as calmly as possible, and hoped he gave a convincing picture of sleep.

His grandfather's footsteps, firm and deliberate, approached along the hall. Nye's door opened, and the dim rays of a shaded lamp added a slight extra glow to the silver moonlight that was already carpeting the room and catching highlights on bedpost and picture frame. Grandfather Kendrick came quietly across the room, and Nye's heart beat faster. He half believed the stern old man would be able to read his guilty thoughts. He could sense his grandfather standing above him, and knew he must be looking down at him.

There were many things Nye might have expected, but he had not expected gentleness. Yet the gentleness of the hand that passed awkwardly over his spiky, tangled hair was unmistakable. Nye heard a deep breath, like a troubled sigh, and then Grandfather Kendrick turned away and went quietly out again. The door closed, winking out the lamp's shaded rays, and left Nye in the semi-darkness of the moonlit room. He sat up in bed, and a feeling of affection and compassion for his grandfather swept over him like a warm wave.

He might never see him again! In another instant he might have called out to him, but then the mood of the moment was shattered like glass by a slight but ominous sound.

It suggested the turning of a key in a well-oiled lock — all mechanisms in Grandfather Kendrick's house were well-oiled and in perfect operating order, from locks to clocks. The footsteps went their appointed way, and the staircase at the end of the hall creaked once again. Nye stared across the room at his door, then sprang out of bed and tiptoed to it. Carefully, striving to make not a sound, he tried it.

It was locked.

Nye backed off from the door, turned, and tottered over to the window seat. If he had suddenly been taken and cast into a dungeon, he could not have felt more lost.

Until now he had not stopped to wonder if his grandfather knew the *Griffin* was sailing in the morning. Now the thought occurred to him at once, and at once he realized that of course his grandfather would know. And in his cautious banker-like way he was making doubly certain that Nye would not put him to the trouble of fetching him back from the waterfront.

Kneeling on the window seat, Nye opened the casement window and leaned out to peer down the red brick side of the house. What he saw made him screw his eyes shut. Seen in the cold glint of moonlight, the sheer drop was terrifying. The ground was dizzyingly remote, and there was not so much as an ivy tendril on the wall to provide a handhold — Grandfather Kendrick held quite correctly that ivy was harmful to brick and mortar.

Nye's lower lip began to tremble. He was close to tears of defeat. Was there nothing he could do? Could he only stay here, a helpless prisoner, and wait for the moment to approach and pass when the *Griffin* would weigh anchor, swing her topsails to catch the first morning stir, and show her heels to England? Head bowed, already kneeling, Nye clasped his hands together desperately and tried to think of a prayer.

"Dear Lord . . ."

Never had a prayer been answered more promptly. Even as he murmured the two words, his mind seemed to be filled with the flash of an idea. There *was* a solution, and he was kneeling on it!

Springing up, he raised the cover of the window seat. One thing Grandfather Kendrick worried about was fire. Every upstairs room was therefore provided with that simple but effective means of escape, a length of rope.

Coiled in the cupboard under the window seat, its end spliced to a ringbolt fastened securely to the flooring of the cupboard, was four fathoms of stout manila line, knotted. Since Grandfather Kendrick had personally tied them, the knots were precisely two and one half feet apart along the entire length of the line. Nye feasted his eyes on the coil and then closed the window seat and began his preparations for leaving.

Out came the drawstring bag, and into it went the few possessions he felt he should take with him: a few pieces of extra clothing, a spare penknife he owned, a small cameo of his mother given him by his grandfather in a solemn ceremony two months ago, a miniature tinted drawing of his father by a Chinese port artist, a pocket purse Cook had given him, with a shilling in it his grandfather had provided, and a few other keepsakes. His packing was soon done, and the strings drawn tight and tied. When he had finished, he put the bag in the window seat and knelt on it again, gazing out and wondering what time it was by now.

"Thank you, Lord," he remembered to mutter, since it seemed no more than right to acknowledge his appreciation for such quick assistance. Now if the Lord would only touch his grandfather's eyes and make him sleepy!

Nye stole over to the door, put his ear to it, and listened. The house was so still he could hear the slow, stately tick of the tall clock on the landing. Surely his grandfather had retired by now! He steeled himself to endure the long wait until the town clock struck ten.

When it seemed as if he could not possibly sit through another leaden minute, and the clock had still not struck, he sprang up and began to dress. Next he took out his drawstring bag and the coil of rope. Another glance out the window, down the side of the house, made him gulp. Rope or no rope, it was a frightening drop. But as he began to pay the rope out the window, he tried not to think about how far below the ground seemed. Finally he tied the cords of his bag together around his neck, and was ready to go.

He took a look around the room, suddenly amazed to think he could really be leaving it. He wondered if for sure his grandfather was asleep, and his throat tightened as he thought of that unexpected show of affection. The memory of that touch made him turn from the window and hurry to his satchel. He found a stubby pencil somewhere in its brown leather depths, took out a sheet of foolscap, and scribbled a note by the light of the moon on the windowsill.

37

Dear Grandfather,
I am sorry. I will miss you.

Your loving grandson,
Nye

And then, a hasty P.S. — *Thank you for the supper.*

He put the note on his pillow, took a deep breath, and turned to the business at hand.

The moment of scrambling over the sill into space, legs dangling helplessly while the rope banged and scraped his knuckles against the hard sill, took all his courage. Then he wrapped his legs around the rope and began to inch down. The sensation of cold, thin air all around him made his stomach scringe, but with each move down the rope his confidence increased. He was careful not to look below, except once. Once was enough.

Slowly he lowered himself past the first floor windows, terrified for fear a light and a face should suddenly appear at one of them. His feet touched ground. He stared once up the full length of the rope, dangling from his window far above, and marveled at his feat. Then he untied the bag from around his neck and was gone without a backward glance. His every thought now centered on the wariness he would need in order to avoid being seen as he slipped from shadow to shadow, making his way down through the silent sleeping town to the waterfront. Somewhere over his head, as he ran, the great clock at long last struck ten.

The air off the water was keen. Nye shivered as he crouched behind a barrel on India Wharf. The bow of an Indiaman in a slip next to the wharf, her bowsprit thrust overhead above the cobblestones, provided a huge curved inky shadow to shelter him from the moonlight. His heart was still pounding from a dozen narrow escapes when he had dived into doorways or darted into alleys to hide from some watchman or late passerby.

Across the way, dim light shone through the dirty windows of the Queen's Tar. From time to time a raucous lifting of raspy voices revealed that the tavern's usual customers were on hand. The cobblestones, black and silver in the moonlight, rang with an occasional rolling step, and once took the alternate thump and slap of a peg-legged sailor's gait as he limped past, but no one stopped to look about as though expecting to find a boy waiting. No one even resembling Mr. Willet came in or out of the tavern. Nye waited in a lather of nervous uncertainty. One moment he felt a surge of confidence, and thought about how he'd like to see old Snodgrass's face, and Dr. Rixby's, when

they heard the news. The next moment he was plunged into gloom, certain that no one would come.

A whistle, low but sharp, made Nye's hair stand on end. The boy with the lank hair hanging across his eyes was standing on the cobblestones not three feet in front of him.

"Just foller me, that's all," he said contemptuously, without a sideways glance, and strolled on.

Fumbling in the darkness for his bag, Nye snatched it up and obeyed. His guide walked to the edge of a wharf, swung over the side and disappeared as abruptly as though he had leaped into the black waters of the harbor. Nye half expected a splash. He hurried to the spot where the boy had disappeared and found a ladder leading straight down into lapping wavelets twenty feet below, where a longboat lay rocking gently against the pilings. Without an instant's hesitation Nye turned and went down the ladder, sure of himself now. A ghastly cough greeted him, a pair of arms reached up and whisked him into the boat, and he found himself staring into twin caverns that even a bright moon could not lighten. Mr. Willet gazed at him with a gloomy sort of respect.

"I knew you'd manage it, if you were your father's son," he declared. "Mind you, they can't call it kidnapping. You came of your own free will, I never approached you, no one can say I ever approached you. Did your grandfather suspect anything?"

"I don't think so," said Nye breathlessly. "I'm sure he was asleep when I left."

"Good. When does he rise?"

"Early."

"Bad. We'll have to hope for a breeze just before daybreak. Will he know you're gone as soon as he's up?"

"I'm afraid he may. I had to leave a rope hanging from my window."

"My word!" said Mr. Willet. He fought down a cough after a brief but exhausting struggle. "You are a plucky one, at that. All right, men, shove off."

There was a limit to Nye's endurance. He was nodding before the longboat reached the *Griffin*, and Mr. Willet carried him aboard. When he opened his eyes again, he was in a berth in a tiny cabin, and when he stared out the porthole there was nothing to look at but daylight and sunshine and blue water.

The *Griffin* had showed her heels to England.

Four

For ten days the ocean was the color of blue enamel under bright September skies. The *Griffin* danced along logging daily runs that were a credit to her. Nye had little to do but run about the ship making friends with all hands. This was not hard, because his father's name proved a passport to openhanded welcome in most quarters. Some of the men had sailed with him, and their respect was immediately evident.

"I shipped out with yer pa that time when we put in at some godforsaken dab o' land or other to fill our water casks — I know 'twas the far side o' the Sandwich Islands — and he faced down the whole blessed tribe o' heathen that was waiting to greet us. We got our water. Oh, a few spears saw us on our way after we shoved off, but nobody took one in his gizzard except a poor little monkey named Higgins, or Wiggins, as I recollect, and he lived."

Several such tales were poured into Nye's ears, some

truer than others, but all adding to his father's stature. In time even the cabin boy — the boy who had brought him the message and met him on India Wharf — unbent enough to talk to Nye occasionally, though he still insisted on treating him as a small and very insignificant boy; all of which seemed perfectly just and fair to Nye, so he didn't mind. After all, as a working member of the crew, the cabin boy *was* somebody to be looked up to.

The only person aboard who did not seem inclined to make friends was a pockmarked, broken-nosed ship's carpenter called Red-Eye Pell — Red Eye because his small squinting eyes were constantly bloodshot. His face, long and swarthy, bore the marks of many a tavern brawl, and some more serious mishap had left him with a noticeable limp. More than that, it seemed to have left him with a permanently soured temper, at least as far as Nye was concerned, because he rebuffed with surly grunts every attempt Nye made to strike up a conversation. On the other hand, Nye caught Pell staring at him once or twice, and though the man always looked away immediately, the glint in the small red eyes was enough to freeze Nye's blood.

When he mentioned to his friend Jerauld, the quartermaster, that Pell did not seem to be friendly, the quartermaster's eyes twinkled with their own hard glint.

"Not likely he would be. You're the wrong breed for him. Four years ago it must be — no, five, I reckon — your pa knocked him down good and proper for his insolence and put him ashore with a kick that sent him halfway to T Wharf, and signed on another man in his place. Had it comin' to him, Red-Eye did — and bein' your pa was skipper, he got what he desarved."

From then on, Nye stayed away from the ship's carpenter. But he was often conscious of the evil red eyes on him.

One other pair of eyes aboard disturbed him. To look up and meet the sunken, brooding eyes of Mr. Willet was like having a dark shadow pass over him. For the first few days Mr. Willet's health seemed almost to be improving, but then his appearances on deck began to be fewer and fewer. On the tenth day the steward told Nye that Mr. Willet had taken to his bunk and was unable to leave it even for meals. Nye thought about going to see him, but the prospect of such a visit was a depressing one, and he kept putting it off.

On the eleventh day the barometer began to drop sharply. The swells became shorter and higher, and the

Griffin began to labor through them, rolling and pitching, under fierce head winds that tore dirty gray clouds to shreds and sent the tatters scudding along as though they were fleeing in panic.

Soon the *Griffin* was in the grip of a thoroughly nasty southwesterly gale that shrieked against shortened sail, clawed the mizzen topsail to shreds, and made every timber in her hull creak and groan from the buffeting. Darkness fell swiftly. Belowdecks the smoky lamps swung in maniacal circles, shedding a checkered light on cabins and galley, forecastle and passageways.

Nye was picking his way along a passageway, heading for the galley, hoping to keep the cook company for a while. He darted forward a few steps at a time and then hung on to the handrail, first on one side of the passageway and then on the other, as the ship rolled and lunged.

Hanging on with his feet braced apart, Nye noticed he was directly across from Mr. Willet's door. It occurred to him to wonder how the poor man might be faring. He decided to knock on the door, as soon as the ship came up from the next roll, and see if Mr. Willet needed anything.

Mr. Willet's cabin was on the starboard side of the passageway. A frightful trough must have opened under the ship, because she rolled to starboard with a violence that put her on her beam-ends. Clinging to the portside handrail, Nye watched the deck tilt down toward the door of Mr. Willet's cabin. With an abruptness that made him start, the door flapped open, and Mr. Willet, half raised in his bunk on one elbow, stared out and up the slant at him with enormous gleaming eyes. Even the black pits could not conceal their wild blaze. The foul lamp swinging overhead sent an unearthly play of light over the wasted, waxen face with its hectic red cheeks. And just before the ship rolled again and the door banged to as sharply as it had opened, Nye saw the man's face contort with horror.

"No! It's a judgment!" he heard him babble from behind the closed door. The sudden vision of the staring invalid had been shock enough to Nye. It was obvious that the equally sudden vision of himself poised almost above the man, framed in the doorway, had been an even greater shock to Mr. Willet. As soon as the ship righted herself, Nye lunged across the passageway, pushed the door open, and peered in.

"Mr. Willet, sir! Are you all right?"

"Don't! Don't come near me!" gibbered the feverish man, drawing back in his bunk.

"But sir, it's only me, Nye Gorham."

47

The frightful eyes burned into him, and then Mr. Willet lay back, exhausted, coughing weakly. When he spoke again, it was in a hoarse murmur, scarcely more than a whisper.

"It's a judgment," he repeated. "I can't . . . can't go . . . with this . . . on my conscience. Your father, boy. Your father!"

A premonition of evil shot through Nye at the mention of his father in such desperately urgent tones. He stepped closer.

"What about my father, Mr. Willet?"

At first Mr. Willet made no reply. It took him a moment to gather strength enough to speak. His mouth

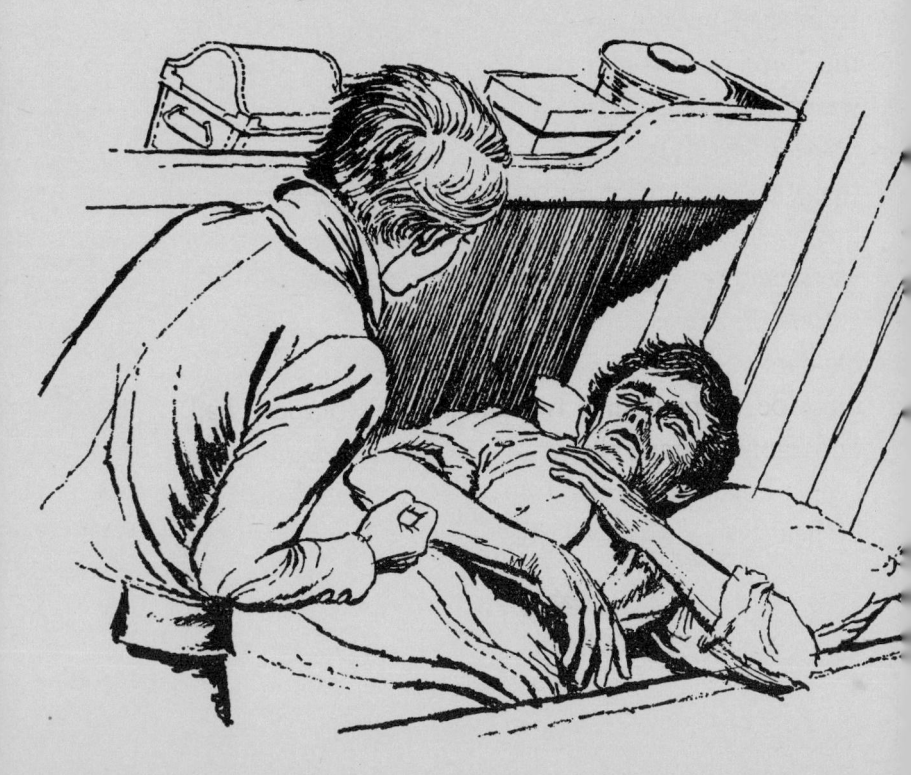

worked, and finally the words came, a thin trickle of whispered syllables.

"Warn him, boy. They plan to . . . kill . . . during voyage . . . new first . . . I know . . . helped . . . cheat . . ."

And that was all. Mr. Willet's eyes drooped shut, his mouth sagged open. Nye felt sure he was dead or dying.

"Mr. Willet! Who's going to kill my father? Who?"

But he could not rouse the invalid. Backing away, Nye stood braced against the bulkhead and tried to believe he had not stepped into a nightmare, that all this was actually happening. In that crazy tip-tilted world of a tiny cabin at sea, where the shadows raced from one corner to another with every pitch and roll of the ship, while the storm shrieked outside and the waxen head lolled on the pillow, nothing seemed real. As he watched, the ghastly face rolled toward him, and then slowly away again. Nye stared at it, feeling faint, but his faintness was caused not so much by what he was seeing as by what he had heard.

One thing was certain: his father was in some terrible danger. Someone was plotting to kill him, and he must be warned. In a twinkling, Nye's purpose had undergone a grave change. Until now, he had simply been a boy looking forward to joining his father. Now he held his father's life in his hands. Only a moment ago, joining his father had been merely something desirable. Now it was absolutely vital.

Who were *they?* If only he could find out that much more from Mr. Willet! He decided to make one last effort. Timing himself with the roll of the ship, he stepped forward and seized the side of the bunk.

"Mr. Willet! *Please,* sir, try to —"

Mr. Willet's eyes were open and staring straight upward, and a thin red line had trickled down his chin from the side of his mouth.

Gasping, Nye stumbled out into the passageway and tried to shout above the clamor of the storm.

"Help!" he cried, struggling toward the galley. "Someone help Mr. Willet!"

Five

WHILE THE *Griffin* was coming into Boston Harbor early one morning three weeks later, there was time for Nye to savor the excitement of being home again at last. Towed by a snorting tugboat with a tall smokestack, the ship slipped past a forest of lofty masts toward her wharf, while Nye, at the rail, reveled in the sight of familiar landmarks. Old South Meeting-house, Faneuil Hall, Old North Church, the State House on Beacon Hill — he would not have been sure of all the names or of which was which without the help of some of the seamen, but he knew them all as old friends.

He had been gone for two years. It seemed like an immense stretch of time, almost too immense to be comprehended. Two years ago he had been living happily with his mother in a handsome old house not far from the Common, with only his father's long absences to cast any sort of cloud over their happiness.

Then his mother's health began to fail. A sea voyage was prescribed, and this fitted well with her own desire to visit Nye's grandfather in England . . . The next two years had held more sadness than joy for Nye. His heart lifted now as his gaze danced across the rooftops from one beloved landmark to another. It was as though his return were bringing to an end that unhappy period of his life, closing the book on it.

The feeling lasted only a moment. Then the dangerous secret he had been guarding and concealing, like some desperate messenger in an enemy land, spread its dark wings again in his mind. It was terrible knowledge to live with alone, but there was no one on the *Griffin* he felt sure of. From the captain on down, those aboard were all strangers to him. How could he know who was to be trusted? His secret lay inside him like a hot iron; he gritted his teeth and bore it. As he thought about it now, he was comforted. In Boston, at least, an ally was waiting, someone who would know just what to do.

"Yonder's where we tie up." A seaman pointed to a long wharf that jutted far out into the water, with a spine of red brick buildings and gray frame warehouses running the full length of it. This time Nye needed no help; he knew every foot of that wharf. He began to strain his eyes for a glimpse of a well-remembered face, his hand half raised in his eagerness to wave the instant he saw his uncle. The ship was being eased alongside the wharf, however, before a small, slim figure, elegant in a black coat, with a black stock at the neck of his frilled white shirt, suddenly emerged from one of the buildings on the wharf in the company of another man.

"Uncle Daniel!" Dancing on tiptoes at the rail, Nye began to wave. Uncle Daniel glanced in his direction, recognized him, and did something so characteristic that Nye laughed until the tears came. His uncle raised his tall hat, as courtly as though he were raising it to a prince — and then waggled it with a teasing smile on his face.

Nye snatched up his drawstring bag, scampered down the ladder from the forecastle, and rushed back to the point in the waist where the gangplank would be run ashore. Heavy hawsers sailed through the air and thumped onto the planking of the dock, the *Griffin* was made fast, and almost before the far end of the gangplank had touched, Nye ran across it into the arms of his uncle.

"Nye, my boy!" Uncle Daniel's face worked strangely for a moment, struggling with some spasm of deep sadness, and then he managed to smile again, and his voice became more hearty. "Lord, how you've grown! Nye, make your manners to Mr. Marshall here. You're walking our way, I believe, Mr. Marshall?"

"I'm just stepping round to Nesbit and Grundy's," said Mr. Marshall as he shook hands with Nye.

"And do you suppose you can still lead the way to the offices of Josiah Gorham and Sons, Nye?" asked Uncle Daniel, cocking his head sideways to inspect Nye with his astonishingly bright-dark eyes.

"Straightaway, Uncle!" Nye all but leaped out ahead in his eagerness to get started. He was bursting with his important, secret news. The sooner they could say good-by to Mr. Marshall and be alone, the better.

"Hold on, now!" His uncle laughed and took his arm. Nye was tall enough now, and his uncle short enough, so that Uncle Daniel hardly had to reach down at all to do so. "Where's Mr. Willet? We'd best wait for him before we go."

"Mr. Willet?" Nye's heart thumped at the name. "Oh, sir, he's dead."

Uncle Daniel's hand tightened convulsively on his arm.

"Dead?"

"Yes, sir. He died one night during the storm."

Slowly the hand relaxed. Uncle Daniel turned troubled eyes toward the ship and shook his head.

"Willet! Poor devil. The mark was on him when he

left, but we had hoped the sea voyage might . . . but apparently he was too far gone. Still, I never dreamed . . . Well, I'm sorry to hear it. He was our good and faithful bookkeeper for over twenty years. Why, he might have died before he even reached England! Well, well. So poor Willet is gone. We need not linger here, then. I'll return later to see the captain and arrange to have his effects brought ashore. Fortunately he had no family."

Hands behind his back, his pointed chin sunk reflectively in the folds of his black stock, Uncle Daniel paced slowly away along the dock, with Nye on one side of him and Mr. Marshall on the other.

"I am thankful to Providence that Mr. Willet survived long enough to call on your grandfather and fetch you aboard the ship, Nye. Tell me, how did you leave your grandfather?"

Nye gulped.

"I climbed out my window," he admitted.

Both men stopped and stared down at him. And then his uncle put his head back and roared with laughter. It was almost surprising to see such a small man laugh so loudly.

"You left him by way of a window, did you?" he said, when he could. "That's not exactly what I meant by my question — I meant to ask if you left him in good health — but that will do. By way of a window. Excellent! An upper-story window, I've no doubt."

"Yes, sir. My bedroom window."

"Better and better! From what I know of your maternal grandfather, I'm not surprised that some unconventional method of leave-taking might become necessary. But pray tell us about it from the beginning."

As they continued along the wharf and turned into the waterfront street on which Nye knew the family offices were located, he told his story. Both men seemed to get considerable amusement out of it.

"A chip off the old block," said his uncle, laying a hand on his shoulder. "A man of action, like his father, and *his* father before him. And with something of their same luck, I'll be bound."

"Keep the luck, my boy, and let everything else go hang," counseled Mr. Marshall, and Nye's uncle was quick to agree.

"Aye, luck, boy, keep the luck. Good luck is half the battle, and bad luck's a double curse, because the world will only call it bad judgment anyway."

They had reached the office. Mr. Marshall patted Nye on the head, shook hands with Uncle Daniel, and continued on his way to Nesbit & Grundy, a marine insurance firm in the next street. Nye followed his uncle upstairs to the second floor offices, above a ship chandler's shop and below a sail loft, and was soon sitting on the edge of a tall teakwood armchair amid the rather gloomy oak paneling of his uncle's private office. The large black lacquered desk his uncle settled himself behind, like Nye's armchair, boasted the fanciful carvings of a Chinese artisan. In a score of ways the room reflected the influence of the China trade. A small display case contained a magnificent ivory carving of a temple, done to the last tiny detail. Flanking this were full-length portraits by Hong Kong port artists of both Nye's father and grandfather, in their ship captain's fittings and looking subtly Oriental about the eyes. These were Nye's favorites of all the paintings in the world. Ordinarily he would have admired them at great length, as he had done dozens of times before when visiting his uncle's office. Now, however, they served to remind him all the more of his vital errand.

His uncle, leaning back in a huge chair that made him seem almost gnome-like, lighted a mahogany-colored cigar and glanced at him keenly through a cloud of smoke.

"Well, now we must consider the matter of posting you on to New York to join your father and the *Ellen*," he began. In the family they referred to the *Ellen Gorham* simply as the *Ellen*.

Nye waited no longer.

"Yes, Uncle, but most of all we've got to warn him right away, because he's in terrible danger!"

Uncle Daniel resembled nothing so much as a relaxed puppet whose strings had suddenly been pulled taut. He sat up straight in his chair, gripping its arms, and stared at Nye.

"Danger? What makes you say that?"

"Mr. Willet told me."

"Willet? When?"

"Just before he died."

Uncle Daniel rose quickly and went to the door. When they had come in, one clerk was out of the office and Nye's uncle had sent the second on an errand. Even so, he glanced out now to make sure he and Nye were alone, then carefully closed the door again. He returned and stood in front of Nye, looking down at him during two deliberate, measured puffs on his cigar. Smoke billowed between them. He waved at it without dispersing much of it, and said, "Nye, tell me exactly what happened."

The smoke made Nye cough. His uncle batted at it again with his hand. Then Nye poured out his story, the story of that stormy night when Mr. Willet lay dying. He had no trouble remembering every detail of what Mr. Willet had said and done — he had already relived the scene a hundred times. His uncle listened without moving a muscle and without once taking his eyes off him, until Nye told about the warning. Then he leaned forward and interrupted, staring almost hypnotically into Nye's wide eyes.

"Once again. Repeat that, now. His exact words."

"He said, 'Warn him, boy. They plan to. Kill. During voyage. New first. I know. Helped. Cheat.'" Nye recited the dying man's warning a bit woodenly, perhaps, but word-perfect.

"That's all he said?"

"Yes, sir."

"Never mentioned names?"

"No, sir. I asked him who was going to kill my father, but then his eyes went shut and his mouth fell open, and blood came out of the corner of it, and he died."

His uncle's lean face twisted as if he were filled with excruciating pain. He turned and went to the window and stood there for a long time, staring out, and twisting his hands together behind his back. Nye waited silently, feeling sorry for him. He remembered what his uncle had said about Mr. Willet — how faithful he had been, and all that. After a while Uncle Daniel came back to Nye and ran his hand gently through the boy's hair.

"Sometimes we have to find ways to excuse betrayal, Nye . . . Willet. That fool! That poor fool, to get mixed up in something, after all the good years he gave us. But it was like him to clear his conscience in the end. We should at least be thankful for that, shouldn't we?"

"Yes, Uncle."

"But 'they'! 'They plan to kill. During voyage.' During voyage! At sea, that is, after they've sailed. Probably make it look like an accident. Or maybe . . ." Nye's uncle straightened and paced away impatiently, up and down the room. "How many 'theys' are there, and who are they?" He stopped in his tracks. "Now, hold on. 'New first.' Of course! That means his new first mate. Your father had to sign on a new first mate for this voyage, man name of Larkins I didn't care for, even though his record is impressive and he knows the China Seas."

Uncle Daniel banged his fist on the desk with a suddenness that raised Nye a foot off his chair.

"Yes, and now I know who another 'they' is! He's the man who talked your father into signing Larkins on! I see this thing now, it's beginning to come clear." He took a puff on his cigar, and paced some more. "The man I'm thinking of is one who's had dealings with your father in Hong Kong. The way things stand now at that end, I can see how it might be to his advantage if your father never got there this trip. We must go down to New York City and warn him at once, Nye."

Nye beamed. He would have liked to get started that very instant. But then his uncle sat down again at his desk and plunged into thought. His face had gone haggard with worry. His cigar went out in his hand, and he laid the stub aside absently on a tray.

"And yet," he muttered, "dare we do that? The man is here in Boston, and he's as wily as a fox. He knows I have some extremely important business to attend to here during the next few days. If I suddenly leave to take you to New York City myself, it might well put him on his guard. It might make him suspect something special had come up . . . No, we must be careful. No sense in catching the small fry in this matter, if we let the real offender slip away . . . If I send you on to New York City, as I might be expected to do, no one will suspect anything."

Uncle Daniel stood up like a man who had come to a decision. He took up his tall hat and put it on. It had the odd effect of making him look shorter instead of taller.

"Nye, I want you to stay here and not talk to anybody until I return. I'm going to make some arrangements. I'll be back as soon as I can."

"Yes, sir."

His uncle was already on his way to the door. His pointed jaw clamped in a hard line, his eyes dark with anger, the small, slender man strode out and slammed the door hard behind him.

For two hours, the longest of his life since the hours in his bedroom at his grandfather's house before his escape, Nye fidgeted about the office, trying to pass the time. Who were the other men in the plot? How many were there? Who was the man Uncle Daniel suspected — the man who had talked his father into signing Larkins on? The man he had had dealings with in Hong Kong? What had happened to make that man want to have his father killed? Something about business, but what? Nye stood in front of his father's portrait, yearning to see him, yearning to be the one who would bring him the all-important warning. If only Uncle Daniel *would* decide to send him on ahead!

The clerk returned from his errand. He tapped on the door to see if Mr. Gorham was in. Nye limited himself to saying he had gone out. The clerk shut the door again and left him alone. Nye wished he could have talked to the man, but remembered what Uncle Daniel had said and dared not.

At last his uncle's quick, light step sounded on the stairs. The office door opened. Despite the energetic way he came in, he looked tired. His face was lined and drawn.

"Well, Nye. I'm sorry to be so long. But everything is settled." He hung his hat on the walnut hat-tree and planted himself before Nye with his hands clasped under his coattails. "While I set a trap here, you're going on ahead to New York City and let your father know what's happened."

"Hurrah!" Nye sprang up delighted.

"Then, when the time comes, we'll spring our trap — there."

Uncle Daniel reached inside his coat and brought out a letter. The envelope was sealed with red sealing wax, and was addressed to *Capt. John Gorham*.

"Here is a letter I have written telling your father how I intend to arrange matters here, and suggesting what should be done there. If all goes well, the man I told you about will come to New York City with me and walk straight into our trap."

"Jolly, Uncle Daniel!"

"Now take off your jacket."

Wonderingly, Nye slipped off his blue pea jacket.

He watched his uncle open a desk drawer and bring out a seaman's sewing kit. With scissors Uncle Daniel neatly snipped the threads of a seam on the inner edge of one flap and slipped the letter inside the lining. He then just as neatly sewed it up again.

"There now. Put that back on, and forget about what's in it until you stand in your father's cabin aboard the *Ellen*."

"Yes, sir. How am I going, Uncle?"

"In the sloop *Plympton Belle*, a coaster leaving in two hours. Now bring your bag and come along — I want to put a good dinner inside you first."

Six

ONE THING Nye could always do was eat. In spite of the excitement he was feeling, he was able to stow away a hearty meal at the excellent side-street tavern his uncle took him to. When they had finished they returned to the waterfront and made their way toward Benson's Wharf, where the *Plympton Belle* lay. She was a good-sized sloop, with trim lines, and looked fast. The last bales of goods had been carried aboard and lowered into her hold. The hatches were being battened down as they went on board. Her captain came forward to meet them.

"Captain Mason, this is my nephew Nye," said Uncle Daniel. Nye looked up at a large man with gray whiskers that seemed to be trying without much success to tone down the fiery redness of his face.

"We'll see him safely there, sir," the captain assured Uncle Daniel. He squinted up at the sky as if it were a mortal enemy. "I'm glad you've come a bit early. I've hurried the men along and we're about ready to cast off. There's talk of bad weather coming up the coast. Sooner we're under way the better. Sooner the better. Tyson! Show this lad where he's to sleep. P'haps you'd like to see, too, Mr. Gorham."

They went below with the seaman to have a look at the cubbyhole where Nye was to sleep. Nye put his drawstring bag on the bunk — the bag was bulkier now, having had a sack of candy added to it by his uncle — and they returned to the main deck. At the gangplank, Uncle Daniel took Nye by the shoulders and gazed down at him intently.

"As soon as I've made sure of the state of affairs here, I'll be coming down to New York City myself. We'll see each other again before this matter is settled and the *Ellen* sails, you may be sure of that. Take care, and don't be afraid. Things will work out."

Nye's uncle gave him a quick squeeze around the shoulders and hurried off down the gangplank. On the dock he turned once, raised his hat and waggled it, but the fun was somehow missing. He clapped his hat on again and walked rapidly away without turning back any more. Nye watched him go with a lump in his throat and felt very much alone. After a glance around to see that nobody was near, he touched his coat, making sure the envelope was still there.

While he was standing by the gangplank, the captain and two seamen came along the deck.

"Mr. Gorham gone ashore?"

"Yes, sir."

The captain nodded. The seamen began to haul the gangplank aboard. From the quarterdeck the mate shouted orders. Sails went up, and lines were cast off. Slowly the *Plympton Belle* gathered steerageway. And Nye's spirits lightened accordingly. After being away from home for two years, he was saying good-by again after only four hours! But what did that matter, and what did a few more days matter, compared to what lay ahead?

The first leg of the passage, across Massachusetts Bay, went well, with the sloop making good use of a strong southwesterly breeze. To the south the sky was becoming rapidly more threatening, causing Captain Mason to mutter ever more anxiously as he scanned it. By the time the ship had rounded Race Point at the tip of Cape Cod, the wind had shifted into the southeast. Gray misty rain blotted out the setting sun and drained its color from the skies. Night fell upon them as swiftly as an assassin, darkness surrounded them like the leaden lining of a coffin. The wind, straight onshore now, howled through the rigging and slatted the

sails as the *Plympton Belle* tried to claw her way out to
sea, away from the fearsome shoals of the Back Side of
the Cape. With grim justice, that treacherous stretch
of sea was called the Graveyard of the Atlantic. It was
a graveyard that numbered its occupants in the thousands.

On such a night there could be no thought of going
to sleep in a black cubbyhole while the ship leaped and
plunged like a maddened creature, when every beam
creaked and shuddered, and every nail shrieked and
groaned as it started in the planking. Staying belowdecks was more than Nye could bear. He found a niche
on the lee side of the main deck amidships where he
could cling to the lifeline that had been rigged along
the length of the deck. He had a deckhouse at his back
to protect him against any wave that might break
across the ship. There he clung to the line for dear life
and strained his eyes across the rearing whitecaps toward the black shore, hoping for a pinpoint of light
from one of the lighthouses along that dread stretch,
and fearing that when he did see one it might be all
too close. Around him, as shouted orders were passed
along by the men, the wind tore scraps of their words
loose and flung them to him.

"It's too heavy . . ."

". . . can't hold her off much longer . . ."

". . . won't answer her helm . . ."

The little he could hear was enough. The men's hurried, labored strides on the pitching deck, the desperate sharpness of their shouts, the last-ditch struggle that went into their efforts to manage the ship — everything the men did, every move they made, told the same story. The ship was in grave danger of being driven ashore. With freezing certainty the hard fact took hold of Nye's mind, and for a moment he was paralyzed. Panic swept over him like a wave, and passed on like a wave, leaving him shaken and still frightened, but no longer unable to think. He remembered his few possessions in his drawstring bag, and felt he must go get them. He never stopped to consider how little chance he would have to save them if the ship struck. He thought only of how precious they were to him. Still clinging to the lifeline, he slipped under it and started to edge aft along the slippery deck.

Out of the storm emerged a shadowy figure, bulky in oilskins and sou'wester, clinging to the lifeline as it came toward him. Nye stopped, wondering anxiously how they could best go about getting around each other. Since he should not be on deck anyway, he knew he must keep out of the way at all times. That being the case, the proper thing for him to do was to retreat back to the deckhouse, where he could duck under the lifeline again and clear it for the seaman. Carefully he edged his way back, planting his feet wide and gripping the line hard with each roll and pitch of the ship.

When he reached the deckhouse, he glanced over his shoulder. The man was closer, and now Nye noticed how he limped. It was a limp that called to mind the ship's carpenter on the *Griffin*, Red-Eye Pell, the man his father had once kicked off his shop for insolence. Nye stared up at the man's face curiously as he came closer — and his mouth fell open.

It *was* Pell!

What was Pell doing on *this* ship? Why would he have left the *Griffin* and signed on the *Plympton Belle* the very day they made port? Why had Nye not seen him until now? The questions seemed to bump and blur one another in their mad race through his mind. Still clinging to the line, Nye stopped in his tracks, too surprised to move on. Seeing him, Pell stopped, too. Strung together on the same lifeline, which neither dared let go, they stared at each other through the howling, spray-filled gloom. Nye's back prickled. Instinctively he shrank from getting too close to the man. Glancing sideways toward the shrouds, he measured the distance, and considered attempting a desperate leap across the rolling, slippery deck. But as he did, the ship dipped into a deep trough, shuddered, righted — and struck.

With a sudden sharp shock, Nye was hurled onto his back. Pell swung violently forward, lost his hold on the lifeline, and vanished in a wild slide ahead along the deck. Nye fetched up in the scuppers with a jolt that knocked the breath out of him, and looked up to see a vision out of a nightmare — a great, bounding, rounded shape that came tumbling and bouncing toward him like some maddened living monster determined to crush him to a pulp. It crashed onto the deck inches in front of him, bounded into the air, and smashed over the railing into the sea. A barrel. A huge hogshead from the deck cargo, brutally heavy, it had been horrible in the way it had seemed bent on destroying him.

The ship righted precariously. Nye struggled to his feet, trying to fight his way back to the lifeline. The ship lay over with a shuddering lurch, and struck again. A wave swept over her and caught him full in the chest. It took him over the side like a mere splinter into a churning maelstrom of pounding water. Something brushed against him, and he flung his arms around it. A spar, a plank, what it was he never really knew, but he hung on, choking and spluttering, while wind and

wave combined to drive it toward the booming surf.

Louder and louder the surf roared and pounded, thunderous now. A tremendous lift, a soaring sensation, a breathless rush forward amid seething waters, and the cruel grate of sand on skin as the wave flung him down. The instinct was instantly strong in him to scramble up and keep staggering, stumbling, crawling forward, even though the frothy lash-tip of each new breaker flogged him to his knees again. Firm sand underfoot at last . . . a few final shaky steps . . . then collapse and oblivion.

Seven

NYE OPENED his eyes on a boundless expanse of whiteness. Boundless at first, but then he looked farther and it became a white plaster ceiling. It became a ceiling which soon, in its travels, met a wall. His gaze, moving down the wall, reached the upper lights of a window, with pale, misty daylight pressing dismally against them. Dropping on down the window, until he was looking straight along the length of the bed he seemed to be in, his gaze finally settled on two faces. Both were bright-eyed though solemn under hair as light as flax. These faces were framed, top and sides, by the lower half of the window. They belonged to a boy his own age and a girl a few years younger. The two children were sitting side by side on a small settle. They were obviously planted there for the express purpose of watching him.

Nye sat up in bed. They took in each other wordlessly. Then the boy bounded off the settle and out of the room.

"Ma! He's awake!" Nye heard him calling with great excitement. "He just waked up!"

The girl smoothed her long gray skirt as demurely as a little old lady, and asked a solemn question.

"What is thy name?"

Nye swallowed, and worked his chin around before replying. His jaw hurt. In fact, now that he was really waking up, he began to discover he hurt all over.

"Nye," he said, and felt of his various bruises.

"Nye. I don't know anybody named Nye. My name is Prudence."

Footsteps and voices coming upstairs proved to be those of the boy and a pleasant-faced woman in a neat, plain dress.

"Well! Good morning, or good afternoon, I should say." The woman took stock of his appearance in a competent and motherly way.

"His name is Nye. I told him mine is Prudence."

"Mine is Tom," said the boy, not to be outdone.

"Don't bother him with names now," said their mother. She laid a cool hand on Nye's forehead, smoothed his hair back out of his eyes, and studied him earnestly. "How does thee feel?"

Nye moved around slightly and grimaced.

"Ooh! I feel — stiff — and sort of sore."

"Small wonder. It's a testament to Providence that thee is alive at all, and thee must give thanks to thy Maker for His goodness."

"How did I get here, ma'am?"

"The men found thee on the beach, and my husband brought thee home."

"What happened to the ship? Did she break up?"

"Not at once. She was driven well in before she went aground for good. Even then she held together for quite a while, and by the grace of the Almighty all but two of those poor souls aboard seem to have been saved."

For the first time, Nye thought of Pell. The man's face sprang up in his mind, sending a thump of fright through him. Instantly he relived that feeling of being caught like a fish on a line. Again he saw the hulking figure and the dark face, felt the sudden shock as the ship struck, and sensed more than saw the threshing bundle of oilskins sliding away into the gloom along the deck . . . It was hard to believe the man had actually been there. There was a confused, dream-like texture about the memory that all but persuaded Nye he had imagined the entire episode. And yet this could not be so. The ship *had* struck, he *had* been thrown over backwards, Pell *had* pitched forward past him . . . But how had Pell come to be there? Why was he aboard the *Plympton Belle?* Why would he have changed ships so soon — and he, a blue-water sailor, ship out on a mere coaster? Or had Pell somehow learned that Nye was going to New York City on the *Plympton Belle?* In short, did Pell have something to do with the plot against his father?

It must be that, Nye decided. Anything else would be too much of a coincidence. Pell hated his father, that much Nye knew. He remembered the way Pell had looked at him on the *Griffin.* If someone was working against his father, Pell was exactly the sort of man who would lend a willing hand.

"Do you know who the men were who were lost, ma'am?"

"No, I'm sorry, but I have no idea."

Two had been lost. Which two? He knew it was wrong to wish another person ill, but if someone had to be missing, he could not think of a better someone for it to be than Red-Eye Pell.

"What is thy whole name?"

"Nye Gorham, ma'am."

"Nye Gorham? Knyvet, that is to say, I suppose."

"Er — yes, ma'am." It was an admission he did not care to make any oftener than was absolutely necessary, but his full given name was indeed Knyvet, pronounced to rhyme with "live it."

"We are the Dillingham family."

"I'm pleased to know you, ma'am." Nye bobbed his head in as good a bow as he could manage under the circumstances. Mrs. Dillingham laughed.

"Thee is a good, polite boy, and for that we'll call thee Nye instead of Knyvet, which may please thee just as well." She held out her hand to Prudence. "Come, Prue, we'll fetch Nye a bowl of soup, and some bread."

Prue went obediently, though it was plain she would have preferred to stay and talk to the newcomer. When they had gone, Tom was able to bring up a more interesting topic.

"They found the two bodies on the beach," he announced with normal relish at being first with the news. "They was drowned."

"Did you see them?" Nye asked quickly.

"No." Tom was sorry to disappoint him, and was disappointed himself. "Pa wouldn't let me. Don't see why, though," he complained. "I saw a man that was shot one time, and that never hurt me any — though of course we don't hold with violence."

"Can you see the ship today?"

Tom nodded. "What's left of her. All the men are

down to the beach gathering what's come ashore of her cargo and fittings and such. Even my father's there. I was a-helping him, too, till he sent me home to see how thee was faring, and if Ma needed any help. We rescued two bolts of tow cloth, and a tin of tea Pa don't think is spoiled, and some good lumber. Some of the men rowed out to the wreck in longboats, and they got even more. How did thee come ashore? Why did thee not stay on the ship, as did most of the others, until they could be taken off?"

"A wave carried me overboard when we struck."

"Then did thee swim?"

"No, I caught hold of something. A plank, I think. Whatever it was, it held me up. I don't remember much about it. I thought I was going to swallow the whole ocean and drown!" Nye looked curiously at Tom. "You talk different," he remarked.

"That's because we're Friends."

"Friends?" Nye wondered what being friends had to do with it.

"Quakers, that is."

"Oh — Quakers. I've heard of those. We had them in England, I think."

"In England? Thee's English? Thee talks different, too."

"But I'm not English. Or anyway, only half. I'm

mostly American, and I'm going to talk like one again as soon as I can," Nye assured him. He was in the midst of explaining about himself when Mrs. Dillingham returned with the soup, followed by Prue carrying a platter of generously buttered bread. The aroma of the soup caused him to break off abruptly and take notice of how hungry he was. While Nye ate his soup and wolfed the thick slices of homemade bread, Tom repeated what he had told him so far. Nye put in a word here and there, but could not bear to neglect his food for long. Each mouthful made him feel amazingly better. By the time he had finished every last morsel, he was able to sit back and tell the rest in a positively chipper tone of voice. Of course he left out any reference to the plot against his father or to Red-Eye Pell.

When he had finished his story, Mrs. Dillingham took the empty bowl and platter and said, "You children may talk to Nye for a few minutes more, and then he must sleep, so that he can soon be himself again."

The children watched her go. Then Prue said, "I have a new kitten named Consideration. Would thee like to see her?"

"No one cares about thy kitten, there's *important* things to talk about," said Tom scornfully. He leaned forward on the settle, one hand planted on each knee, and asked Nye a deep question. "How does thee stand on Abolition?"

Nye blinked at him.

"On what?"

"Abolition!"

"What's that?"

"It's abolition of slavery. Look 'ee, does thee believe Negroes should be slaves?" asked Tom, getting down to plain terms. Both children waited breathlessly while Nye considered.

"Well, I've never had much cause to think about it," he admitted, "but — well, I'm certainly not *for* it . . ."

"Then thee's against it!"

"I don't think *anybody* should be a slave," Nye decided.

"Then thee's an Abolitionist!"

"Well, I guess I am," agreed Nye, surprised to find he was something he had not even known about.

"Tom! Thee's going to tell him!" cried Prue, wide-eyed.

"Well, why not? If he's an Abolitionist, he won't tell anybody else, will he? Well, then!"

"Tell me what?"

After exchanging a glance, Tom and Prue rose and

came closer. Tom looked important, Prue looked excited. Tom's voice dropped to a conspiratorial whisper.

"We're a station on the Underground Railroad!"

Nye was not much better off with the Underground Railroad than he had been with Abolition.

"What's the Underground Railroad?"

"It's to help runaway slaves get safe to Canada. Mostly they travel at night, so they have to have places to hide in the daytime, especially when some vile slaveowner is chasing them and is close on their trail. Last year Pa went to visit some of our people in Ohio, and that's where he got the idea. He came home and built one just like it."

"Like *what?*"

Tom and Prue exchanged a delicious glance, looked this way and that as if expecting vile slaveowners' spies to pop out of the woodwork, and came even closer alongside the bed.

"A secret passage!"

"A tunnel!" whispered Prue.

"Well, both!"

"I say! You mean, you have a secret passage? In *this* house?" Nye did not mean to sound impolite, but he did not get the feeling he was in a large house, like the great houses in England, where there was plenty of room for secret passages and everybody expected them to be there.

"Yes! And what's more" — another glance exchanged by Tom and Prue, beside herself with bubbling excitement now — "the secret entrance to it is right here in the spare room!"

"Really?" Nye's eyes darted about the four walls. "How jolly!"

"It's not out here. It's in the closet. All a body has to know is which board to push, and — whist! — away he goes!"

Tom's description set them all laughing.

"That's first-rate, that is," declared Nye. "How many runaway slaves have you hidden so far?"

Tom's laughter faded. His face grew pink with embarrassment. Obviously Nye had touched on a sore point.

"Well, so far, not any," he admitted with a pathetic sigh. "So far not any have come this far down-Cape. But Pa keeps hoping. And we're ready when they *do* come."

They talked for a while about how unfair it was for runaway slaves not to run in the proper direction — by way of the Dillingham farm, that was to say — and then Mrs. Dillingham put the threatened end to their conversation by calling upstairs to say it was time for Nye's nap.

"Of course thee must tell nobody about our Underground Railroad station," Prue whispered before they left.

"Unless thee happened to meet a runaway slave," Tom added wistfully.

"If I do, I will. Otherwise, I won't," Nye promised.

Left alone, he settled back against the pillows and dutifully considered Mrs. Dillingham's theory concerning sleep. But he was still thinking about runaway slaves being pursued by a vile slaveowner. And when he pictured the slaveowner, whip in hand, he was startled to find he looked exactly like Red-Eye Pell. Thoughts of Pell took him back to the reason he had been aboard the *Plympton Belle* in the first place, and at last his predicament hit him full force.

What was he to do now? How was he to get to New York City? His father still had to be warned just as much as ever! He could not simply lie here and —

Nye actually started to jump out of bed. But then a certain draftiness about the legs reminded him of a crushing handicap. He didn't have any clothes! He did not even know where his clothes were, and wherever they were they must still be soaking wet. What was he to do? And his letter! His precious letter! It was soaked and probably ruined!

For a moment he was so wretched and lost he had to fight back tears. But then he caught hold of himself by remembering he was no longer without friends. If Mr. Dillingham was anything like Mrs. Dillingham and Tom and Prue, Nye was among good people. Quakers were *known* to be good people, anyway. And if that was the case, then he could talk to Mr. Dillingham, and Mr. Dillingham would help him. At once Nye felt a surge of confidence, a feeling that things would work out. Even though his letter was soaked, perhaps his father would still be able to make out some of it. And if not, Nye could at least put him on his guard by telling him about Mr. Willet and warning him about his new first mate, Mr. Larkins.

Feeling more at ease again, Nye allowed his thoughts to return to the wreck. He found an unhappy fascination in trying to imagine how the *Plympton Belle* must have looked, out there on a sandbar with her hull cracked open and her cargo spilled out of her hold into the water, to be washed ashore, rolled and shoved by the waves, or be covered over by sand somewhere along the way.

His drawstring bag! His loss struck him like the blow of a fist. His bag with his pictures in it, his beautiful cameo of his mother, and his miniature of his father! They were gone. They were lost forever.

Nyc had not cricd whcn Pcll had fillcd him with mortal terror, and he had not cried when he found himself wondering how he would ever get to New York City now; but when he remembered his pictures, he cried.

Up, up, up out of a black well of deep, restoring sleep came Nye into a room that was now dusky-dark. As he sat up and stretched, there was just enough of a lighter shade of gray coming through the window to show him a neat pile of clothing on the settle.

His clothes! They were all washed and dried by the fire and ready to put on again. Everything was there but his shoes and stockings. Leaping out of bed, Nye picked up his jacket. He could feel the bulk of the letter still inside the lining. He was tempted to find out what condition it was in, but he had no knife, and besides that, he knew he should not take it out of its safe hiding place. He began to dress. Nothing could have done more for his morale. Now he felt the battle was half won before it had even begun. As soon as Mr. Dillingham came home, he would tell him everything and ask him to help.

Standing at the window while he dressed, he

watched wisps of fog swirl over the dunes that lay between the house and the steep bank that dropped to
the shore. The wind had died away almost completely.
A heavy fog was silently rolling in from the sea like a
gray blanket, covering all in its path. As he was button-
ing his shirt, Nye pressed his face against the window,
peering intently into the gloom, and began to smile.
Here came some men now, up over the dunes, heading
this way, which probably meant Mr. Dillingham was
one of them. Three figures there were, moving in and
out of swirls of fog like wraiths, half-seen one moment,
disappearing entirely the next.

Nye's smile froze on his face. His hand froze on
the button it was fumbling with, his heart froze in his
breast. Again and again puffs of fog wrapped like
shrouds around the three figures on the dunes, and
again and again they burst through their wrappings
like escaping mummies. And each time they did, Nye
saw that the front figure was walking with a limp. An
unmistakable, all too familiar limp.

Eight

WHY WAS Pell coming here? Nye pulled on his jacket and watched the men stop not far from the house. They put their heads together for a conference; then Pell left them and came on alone. One of the other men disappeared into the fog. The second one stationed himself almost directly in front of Nye's window, near the shed door. It was as though they meant to make sure no one slipped out of the house unseen.

A heavy-handed knock sounded on the door downstairs. Nye could hear the children calling their mother. He could hear her asking who it was, and Pell saying, "It's one of the men from the wreck, Miz Dillingham, come to see about the Gorham lad. I'm responsible for him, ma'am. I have papers, all notarized in proper legal fashion, as puts him in my custody for the voyage, so I've been mighty uneasy about him till I learned he was here safe and sound."

Papers, all notarized in proper legal fashion! Nye

was not even sure what that meant, but he was certain about one thing — it meant that Pell had some sort of papers that would look right and fool people. But why would he have such papers? There could only be one answer. Pell *did* have something to do with the plot against his father.

Nye felt hideously trapped. He wanted to stay clear of Pell, yet how could he do it? He gasped for breath as though he were being strangled, and stared wildly about the room. And then he all but said aloud the magic word that shot up in his mind like a sky rocket.

Abolition!

Yanking open the closet door, he rushed into its black interior and began pawing the wide boards that lined it, pushing hard on this one and that. Downstairs, Pell's voice was booming away inside the house now, jovially asking Mrs. Dillingham to lead the way. His heavy, uneven step began to make the stair treads creak behind her.

Despair closed around Nye as each tread creaked outside and each board held firm inside. Furiously he kicked a board — and clamped his jaw shut to stifle a howl of pain. The board had swung away at the bottom, and the top had hit him painfully on the head. The board was hinged in the middle.

Ducking down, Nye wriggled through the opening.

Once through, he stood up and pushed the board back into place. At that instant a dim hint of light through the crack told him that Mrs. Dillingham had led the way into the room carrying a lamp. She was saying, "He may still be asleep, but . . . Why, he's not in his bed! Now, where is he?"

Dim as it was, such of the lamp's light as slanted into the closet and seeped through the cracks between the boards was enough to break the total darkness Nye had found himself in. It showed him a steep and narrow flight of steps. Glad he was barefooted, he stole silently down them into ever-deeper blackness, feeling his way at each step, smelling damp, musty earth at the bottom. When he felt dirt under his feet, he dropped to his knees and pawed around him with hands that shrank away from what they might touch. They encountered crumbly earth everywhere except straight ahead. He edged forward. He could sense damp soil close around him and close above his head. He was crawling through a tunnel in the earth, a tunnel that led to — what, he didn't know. The boom of Pell's voice, still coming to him in hollow, muffled, far-off tones, forced him on through the dreadful dark clinging dampness. The slightest rustle or scrape around him put his heart in his mouth. Anything could be in that tunnel. Any sort of creature, any slimy, creeping thing, could be waiting to attack him in the utter blackness.

"So!"

Nye's teeth chattered in a spasm of blind fright. Pell sounded close enough to touch him.

"Here's where he slipped through! Where does this lead to, ma'am?"

Pell had found the loose board, and the tunnel carried his voice like a speaking tube. The sound seemed to envelop Nye.

"Lad! Come out of there, now!" Pell called in wheedling tones, striving to sound kindly. "Don't make poor old lame Pell crawl down there after you!"

Nye scrambled forward recklessly — and ran into solid earth. The tunnel had come to an end! It was like climbing into a grave to be buried alive. Suddenly there was nowhere to go.

Boom!

His heart nearly stopped beating. A thunderous crash had sounded directly over his head. After that first fright, as a second crash followed, he knew he was hearing footsteps straight above him. Reaching up, he touched wood. A wooden floor! The escape hatch of the tunnel, it must be — and someone was standing on it!

Now he was surely lost. Any second now one of the men would pull up the trapdoor and find him. A shout came from the house.

It was Pell again, still trying to keep up his masquerade of joviality.

"Mates! I found a passage here out o' the house, and the lad's crawled through it. It comes out over by the big tree yonder, the good wife says, so step over and lay him by the heels before he cuts away and comes to some harm."

Wood creaked over Nye's head. Then all was silent. The man had left. Mrs. Dillingham, bless her, had told them the wrong place! With hands and then shoulders Nye pressed against the wood overhead. It was heavy, cruelly heavy, but with the strength of desperation he forced it up. Wisps of straw fell down on him as he worked. It was some of the straw that liberally covered the floor — and the hatch, to conceal it. Scrambling up through the opening, he found himself in a small barn. The barn door hung open. Nye could hear the voices of the men close by. Carefully he peeped out. They were not fifty feet away, over by a big tree, examining the ground. The fog was perversely thin in that direction. He saw them with frightening clarity for an instant before a gray veil partially obscured them.

To step out of the barn with the men so near took the full measure of Nye's courage. If the fog drifted clear again, if one of them happened to glance around, if he made so much as a sound . . . Holding his breath, he began to edge outside. On tiptoe he made a rush for the corner of the barn.

"Where's the blasted opening?" Pell was growling as he scrabbled at the earth. "Blast it, we need a lamp!"

Nye eased around the corner. He began breathing again. Now, with the barn between him and the men, he could start to pick his way through the night and get away. After the total darkness of the tunnel, even the foggiest of nights would have seemed less obscure. Even so, he could not see enough to go more than a step or two at a time. Vague, ghostly shapes loomed up at him when he was almost on top of them. Once he ran straight into a tree. The worst came, however, when his hand, feeling in front of him, bumped the side of a woodpile and sent several lengths of stove wood rattling down its side. The sound was like a ragged volley of muskets.

"Ahoy there! What's that?" Pell's voice, behind him, was like a hand at his throat. "That's him! After him!"

To be chased in the fog was nightmarish, because he dared not run. That would only mean smashing himself up in one way or another, and that was the surest way of all to get caught. But at least the men could not run, either. Behind him he heard them howl and curse as they stumbled into potholes or tripped over roots. Except for the one near the house that he had run into, Nye never came upon a tree; nothing but low bushes on rolling, sandy hills that sloped down into deep depressions. He stumbled on and on, straining up pebbly slopes on one side, slipping and sliding down their sandy sides on the other. Gradually the men's voices blurred in the distance. They seemed to have lost all track of him. But Nye kept going, even after he could hear them no longer, simply because he was too frightened to stop.

At the same time, his legs were beginning to tremble under him as his strength, hardly back to normal after his battering of the night before, began to fail. Beads of sweat chilled his skin as they rolled down his face, each one telling a dangerous story of how near he was to exhaustion. He was tottering when his hand came flat against the roughness of old white-cedar shingles. Nye leaned hard against them, panting, wondering in a half-dreamy way what stood in his path now, and too spent to try to move around it. He looked up and saw the shingled side of a shed looming up out of the fog, stretching away in both directions, disappearing mistily overhead. A shed. A hiding place. He was ready to accept it for better or worse. He was at the end of his tether. Feeling his way to a door, he staggered inside and found a pile of salt hay waiting invitingly in a stall with a hearty animal smell about it. He was asleep almost before he touched the hay.

Red-Eye Pell was prodding him in the ribs. Standing over him with blazing blood-red eyes full of evil triumph, Pell was prodding him sharply in the ribs and roaring, "Well! What have we here?"

Nye twitched violently. His eyes flew open. Instead of Pell, he found himself staring up in gray morning light at a short, stocky figure with popping blue eyes set in a leathery old face trimmed with a low hedge of grizzled whiskers. Everything about the old man's face was broad. The eyes were held well apart by the broad bridge of the wide, stubby nose that flared under it. The mouth was wide, and squared off by determined lines at each end. The chin was broad and square beneath its spiky covering of whiskers. And the whiskers were bristling with indignation.

"What are you doing, sleeping in my ox stall? Why, you must be —Out with it, young scalawag!" he ordered, giving Nye one more poke in the ribs with the

butt end of the pitchfork he was holding. He stood it aside and hauled Nye to his feet by the collar. "Ain't ye the young 'un as was over to the Dillinghams', and run away last night, and had grown men hallooing up and down the face o' the earth looking for him in a pea-soup fog, and all for what, that's what I'd like to know, and for what?"

It was undoubtedly the longest question Nye had ever been asked, and seemed to end when it did only because the asker ran out of breath.

"Yes, sir, I am," Nye admitted, "but please, sir —"

"Then back ye go to the Dillinghams', and we'll get the straight of it there!" declared the old man, tugging his timeworn sea captain's cap down over his contentious eyebrows with one hand and tugging Nye along with the other.

"No, please, sir!" Nye pulled back so violently that his jacket almost parted in the old man's grasp. "Don't let them see me!"

"Don't what? Now, why on earth shouldn't John Dillingham —"

"Not him, sir! Those men!"

The old man swung around full on and peered fiercely into Nye's face, his blue eyes popping more than ever.

"Hey? What about those men? What's wrong with

those men, poor beggars as they are from a ship pounded to pieces on the devil's own shoals, and wanting no more'n to fetch a lad they was accountable for?"

This second longest question in Nye's experience gave him time to consider what he could do to convince the man of the seriousness of his plight. He decided the only way to do it was to tell the whole story of what had happened to him, without reservation. For despite the old man's irascible manner, Nye had a feeling there was more smoke than fire involved, and that behind the smoke screen might stand a fair man. At any rate, he had little other choice. He could not keep on running, friendless and alone, even if he could get away again. Not if he was ever to reach his father.

"Sir, if you'll give me a chance, I'll tell you all about what's wrong with them. My name is Nye Gorham, and I'm from Boston, only I've been living in England for two years with my grandfather, but after my mother died —"

"Hold on! This going to be a long yarn?"

"I'm afraid so, sir."

"Hmp!" His audience looked around, found a barrel he could kick out of a corner, and sat himself down on one end of it, folding his arms sternly. "Gorham, hey? Good Boston name."

"My father's a ship captain," said Nye. The old

man's cap provided him with an inspiration. "Maybe you're one, too, sir?"

"Was," he snapped, but looked not displeased to have the fact recognized. "Was, for nigh on forty years. Not a blue-water man, but Cap'n Shebnah Berry nonetheless. Go ahead. What's all this about your being from Boston and living among the scoundrelly British for two years and your poor mother dying, which is more of a lump to be thrown at a man's head all at once than anyone in his right mind could begin to comprehend? Start at the beginning, lad, and pay it out slowly!"

Carefully Nye started all over again. With the aid of an occasional question, some of them relatively brief, he was able to put the facts before Captain Shebnah in reasonably good order. When he had finished, the old man stared at him hard for a while and then rose to his feet shaking his head.

"I've heard some wild yarns in my day, but yours comes close to beating the lot of 'em. It's a hard one to swaller. Your uncle, now, sending you on to New York City aboard the *Plympton Belle*. If 'twas important to get you there, that wasn't the fastest way to send you, not by a danged sight. Why, the boat train to Fall River and a steamboat from there would have got you to New York City next morning! And this feller Pell being in on some plot, that's a hard one to swaller, too. You've been through an unsettling experience, getting washed ashore from a wreck. I'm not sure it hasn't unsettled your mind a mite!"

In his moment of need, with Captain Shebnah's skeptical blue eyes boring into his, Nye again remembered his letter. He slapped his jacket.

"Well, if you won't believe me, maybe you'll believe my Uncle Daniel!"

"Hey? What do you mean, lad?"

"My uncle wrote a letter to my father, telling him who he thought was in on the scheme to do him harm, besides the new first mate. He gave it to me to take to my father, and it's right here in my jacket! It got wet, but it's still there, and maybe you can make out some of it if you look at it."

Captain Shebnah eyed Nye narrowly.

"And where might it be?"

"It's sewed inside."

"It's what?"

Nye opened the flap of his jacket and pointed to his uncle's precise needlework. The captain inspected it silently. Then he produced a penknife. His blunt, hard thumbnail prised open the stubborn blade.

"Let's have a look."

Nye held the flap open. Captain Shebnah ran the

blade neatly up the ladder of stitches, and felt inside the lining. He brought out the ruins of a once-white envelope, crumpled and stained, and with only traces of its sealing wax remaining. Nye groaned.

"The writing's all gone from the outside!"

"Well, of course it is! What did you expect ink to do, after such a dousing?" Captain Shebnah peered more closely at the envelope, and added, "Not altogether gone, at that. There was a name on it, all right, and that name could have been Gorham," he admitted.

"Open it up, sir! Maybe you can make out some of my uncle's writing inside, if it isn't too spoiled."

"Well, I don't much enjoy opening another man's mail, like a certain postmaster does that I happen to know not a stone's throw from here," growled Captain Shebnah, "but under the circumstances I don't see no other way out. No other way of getting to the bottom of things . . ."

"You're not really opening it, anyway, sir, because it's already open," Nye pointed out helpfully, and in truth the pages were half falling out of the unstuck remains of the envelope. Captain Shebnah gave him a reproving glance.

"I'm opening it," he replied, in tones worthy of Moses handing down the Ten Commandments. "The minute I unfold pages as was intended for other eyes, I'm opening another man's . . ."

Meanwhile he was unfolding them, and as he did so his comment died in mid-air. He held the pages out from him, then brought them close. He inspected them one by one with growing astonishment. And Nye, at his shoulder, stared at them with much the same feelings. They exchanged a completely bewildered glance.

"Dousing or no dousing," spluttered Captain Shebnah finally, "this don't look right. No, by the blazes of Tophet, it don't look right to me. If I'm any judge of the matter, these sheets o' writing paper never had a word written on them at all!"

Nine

NYE'S HEAD REELED from trying to grasp this senseless new development. If Captain Shebnah had not
been there, he might have made himself believe that
a thorough soaking in both salt and fresh water could
wash ink out of paper without leaving a trace. But
Captain Shebnah Berry did not believe it, and Nye
could not believe it either.

"But, sir," he said, as they stared at each other,
"why would my Uncle Daniel give me a letter to take
to my father with nothing written on it?"

The old man looked away, and down at the letter.

"It's beginning to make more sense now," he muttered. His lips moved as though some of the things he
was thinking of saying had put a bad taste in his
mouth. He folded the sheets carefully, put the envelope around them, and laid them aside on a shelf. Then
he rose and took a bandy-legged turn up and down
the shed. He stopped, tugging at his whiskers on one

side in a sharp way that made his cheek bulge out like an old leather pouch, and studied Nye.

"What kind of feller is this Uncle Dan'l of yours? Tell me about him. Is he a seagoing man, like your pa?"

The question sparked a memory. It was a memory that went back nearly a year, before his mother died. He saw her, pale and wasted, but still able to smile when he came into her room for his daily visits. He could see the blue veins traced on her beautiful, delicate hands as they lay on the white bed linen, and hear her voice, hardly more than a whisper but still firm. Sometimes they had talked for a long time in those days, about all sorts of things, about everybody and everything. And Captain Shebnah's question had stirred the memory of a question of his own. He could hear himself asking it:

"Ma, why doesn't Uncle Daniel be a ship captain like Pa?"

He could remember how his mother, smiling with a queer sort of sadness, had replied.

"I asked my mother about that once," he told Captain Shebnah. "She said Uncle Daniel went to sea when he was younger, but he didn't seem cut out to be a ship-handler like Pa. She said Grandpa Gorham decided Uncle Daniel had better stay home and tend to the business side of things. Grandpa said somebody had to do that, anyway."

Captain Shebnah moved his tongue around in his mouth and made a slight face, as if the bad taste were still there, bothering him.

"So your uncle stayed home and took care of the business, and your father sailed the ship."

"Our best ship, yes. We've four others, too, but the *Ellen Gorham*'s our best."

"Your flagship, hey? I see. Four others. The *Griffin* is one of those?"

"No, sir."

"Hmm. But it was your Uncle Dan'l as sent this Mr. Willet over to fetch you for your pa — this Mr. Willet who, by his own confession on his deathbed, helped cheat your pa in some manner, shape, or form. Him as was the head bookkeeper, working in your uncle's office. And your Uncle Dan'l it was as sent you on, putting you on board the coaster to carry the news to your pa. He did that instead of sending you the quickest way or, better yet, bringing you himself. Of course, his story about having to stay in Boston sounded likely enough to you at the time. And as far as you knew, coming by coaster was as quick as any other way — ain't that right? You wouldn't have known any different."

This was true, of course. All those things his uncle had said in his office about some other man, all the thinking he had seemed to do to work out a plan — had that all been mere playacting, meant to deceive Nye? Unwilling to believe it, Nye searched for an explanation.

"Maybe there was some special reason why he wanted to send me on a coaster. And anyway, he didn't know she would be shipwrecked!"

"That's true enough," agreed Captain Shebnah, "but he *did* know she was planning to touch at Nantucket, and be delayed there awhile."

"What?"

The captain nodded. "That's what I hear tell her skipper said. Almost appears as if you wasn't supposed to get to New York City with your news in time to do any good," Captain Shebnah went on relentlessly. The way his lips were pursed now, there was no question about the bad taste that was bothering him. "Why did that feller turn up on the *Plympton Belle* — that Pell feller? He didn't just happen to be there — I'm willing to admit that now. He was there because your uncle went to the *Griffin* and got him and *sent* him on board her. He wanted somebody to keep an eye on you. And finally, it was your Uncle Dan'l as gave you a letter to your pa with nothing written in it."

"But why? Why would he do that?"

"What else could he do? There wasn't really any story for him to give you to tell your pa, unless he made one up, and made up some names for the men he was pretending to suspect. A dummy letter was a much easier way out, and bound to impress you more, too. It could have been awkward later on, too, for you to know a bunch of false names."

If Captain Shebnah had been stringing Nye up by the thumbs, it could hardly have hurt worse. The old man could not have made shrewder conjectures than he had in the matter of the letter. How impressive and important it had looked, with its red sealing wax! Nye remembered how he had wondered about the other men in the plot while he was waiting in his uncle's office, how he had wondered if his uncle would tell him who they were. He would have asked about them at once, when he knew he was going to New York City, if his uncle had not produced the letter . . . But his Uncle Daniel! How could he believe anything bad about his Uncle Daniel, whom he had always loved and respected, and who loved him — Nye was sure he did! Uncle Daniel had always been good to him, and good to his mother, and . . .

"I don't see how my uncle could do it!" he groaned. "I just don't see!"

"Aye, it's a bad world sometimes, and we can't always understand why," the old man muttered. "Jealousy, now. Jealousy can do terrible things, terrible, terrible things."

"Jealousy?"

The captain nodded. "Grown-ups get het up about things sometimes that wouldn't make much sense to a boy. But when you're older you'll understand."

Nye hung his head, and shook it bitterly. "I'll never understand. Never!"

"Hmm." The captain's voice sharpened. "Well, be that as it may, we'd best stop dillydallying and start doing something about getting you along to your pa."

Nye's head came up.

"You'll help me?"

"Course I'll help ye!"

The words were what Nye needed. They gave him the spirit to remember that, no matter what Uncle Daniel was or was not, there was his father to think of first.

"Thank you, Captain!"

"Now, let me see, how do we go about this?"

"Can we send a message to Pa right away?"

The captain tugged at his cheek. He looked dubious. He stared into space, and what he said next made it plain that he was calling on his own experience to visualize what the situation might be at the other end, aboard the *Ellen Gorham*.

"Don't know as that would be best, lad. But let's consider all the various possible schemes, to begin with. First, there's the mail. Well, *you* could get there afore a letter would from these parts as was sent by the mails. Next, as for getting someone to take a message — by horseback, let's say, other ways overland being too slow — I don't know who we could find to go. Ain't a soul in these parts as wouldn't look on going to New York City the way they'd look on a trip t'other side o' the moon. Bangkok, now, or Madagascar, or China — that's nothing. But New York City!

"There's another thing to think about, too. When a ship's in port, getting ready to sail, but not fixing to leave fer a few days, the skipper's likely to be ashore a good deal of the time. It's the mate who's more likely to be aboard, supervising the loading of her. And if this new first mate o' your pa's is a bad 'un, that could make for a ticklish situation, unless the messenger was mighty clever about his work. Wouldn't want that mate to get hold of the message first, would we?"

The captain bent his gaze in Nye's direction, studying him.

"However, that don't make no matter, anyway, because I've an idea for getting you there yourself as fast as any living soul could make it, if all goes well. You've managed to come all this way from England, you're capable of going the rest of the way, once you're told how."

"Aye, sir! How can I do it?"

The captain perched on his barrel again.

"Jabez Snow will be sailing across the bay to Plymouth this morning. If the wind holds steady and in its present quarter, he'll be there in time for the stage to Fall River. The stage gets to Fall River in time for the steamboat that waits for the boat train from Boston. And that steamboat will dock in New York City tomorrer morning —"

"Tomorrow *morning!*"

Captain Shebnah smiled at his excitement. "Lucky fer you I was cap'n of a packet myself, going to Boston and now and then to Plymouth, or I might not know such connections was even possible. Now, here's what we'll do. Jabez will be sailing before long, so you've got to get down there to the harbor as fast as you can. Now, Belshazzar's too slow — Belshazzar's my ox there — and I've got a leg as gives out on me if I walk any sort of distance. But you're a spry lad, you can get down there in no time, specially along the path I'm going to show you.

"Pamet Harbor, that's where you're going. It's on

the bay side o' the Cape, which is the opposite side from the one you was wrecked on, the Back Side. Naturally, it would have to be on the bay side, fer you to go to Plymouth, because Plymouth's almost straight across the bay, about four hours' sail fer Jabez. If you don't let no grass grow under your feet, you'll be down there before Jabez hoists sail. I'll just go into the house fer a minute, and then we'll head for that path. You keep out o' sight, and wait here."

Nye watched Captain Shebnah roll outside with his bandy-legged walk to a large-wheeled cart with a huge ox standing between the shafts. For the first time Nye became truly aware of the fuzzy gray light and keen fresh air of early morning. The old captain cast an eye this way and that, as though satisfying himself about the state of the weather and the probability of the haze "burning off" in an hour or two, which — according to what he said to Belshazzar — it generally did. Nye understood that actually he was having a look around to make sure nobody else was in sight. Having done so, Captain Shebnah glanced back at Nye, nodded, and then disappeared into the house.

Ten

WHILE HE WAITED, Nye peeped out of the shed at Captain Shebnah Berry's gray-shingled, white-trimmed cottage and wondered exactly where he was. And how far was it to the harbor he would be sailing from? Back in England, Nye had spent many a homesick hour poring over an atlas of his grandfather's, admiring a map of America, and dreaming of a time when he would return there. Massachusetts had looked quite small on that map, but even now he could remember almost every detail of its shape and situation.

He could remember the squiggly way Cape Cod curled out into the ocean, looking like an arm bent at the elbow. He could remember the star that stood for Boston, the state capital. He was hazy as to the exact location of the few other towns that were shown — Fall River, for instance. He could not remember where Fall River was located. But he could remember Plymouth. As Captain Shebnah had said, it was on the

shore, straight across the bay to the west from Cape
Cod. Closing his eyes, he could see the dot with *Plymouth* printed beside it. He could remember the way
the coast of New England swung to the west below
Cape Cod, and he knew New York City was at the
bend where the coastline went south again. It was
south and west of Cape Cod, then, but how far? Not
too far, surely, if he could get there on a steamboat by
tomorrow morning.

In a moment Captain Shebnah came out of the
house snapping shut a worn leather coin purse. He had
part of a loaf of bread under his arm. He came into the
shed and handed the purse to Nye.

"Wish I had more ready money on hand, but I
reckon you can make do with what I've managed to
scratch together. Put this in your pocket, and take care
of it."

"Thank you, Cap'n!" Nye thrust it deep into his
jacket pocket. "I'll see that you get it back, sir."

The captain nodded. "And take this, too. You're
probably hungry."

"Aye, sir!"

"Then hang onto it, and eat it when you can. Now,
then, we'll let Belshazzar take us, with you under the
canvas in the back o' the cart, till we get to the path,

which ain't but a hop, skip, and jump from here. There's a few things in the cart — odds and ends I and Cap'n Zeb picked up down to the beach. In fact, if 'twasn't that I and Belshazzar stayed the night at Cap'n Zeb's, it setting in so foggy, you'd have had him for a stall-mate last night.

"But anyways, there's still room enough fer you in the back of the cart, and that's where you'd best travel, just in case we fetch up with that Pell feller somewheres along the way. According to what you say he told Miz Dillingham, he claims he has you in his charge, with papers to prove it. And from what we know now, I don't doubt he has. I don't doubt your uncle provided him with just such papers. Pell would have the law on his side, and there'd be little I could do about it. Our own constable would have to turn you over to him, if he had the proper papers to show. So wait here, and I'll make sure there's room to stow you away in."

Captain Shebnah walked out to the cart and turned back a corner of the square of ancient sail canvas, dark with mildew, that covered the stake body of the cart. After peering under the canvas, he jerked his head, and Nye ran out beside him. Before boosting Nye up to climb in, Captain Shebnah pointed to a chimney and one corner of a roof that showed themselves over a low, rolling, sandy slope sparsely covered with bushes and brush. Near the house the top branches of a solitary tree were also visible.

"You see that house over there? That's the Dillinghams'."

Nye stared, sure that Captain Shebnah was fooling.

"The Dillinghams'? But that house is so close, and I walked for miles and miles."

The old man chuckled in his beard. "Maybe it felt that way, and maybe you *did* walk quite a piece, but out in that fog, and not knowing where you were going, you probably walked round in a circle. I expect you fetched up here from t'other side of the property," he said, pointing across the cart in the opposite direction.

He had hardly finished pointing, and Nye was standing on tiptoe for a look, when they heard sounds coming from that vicinity. Captain Shebnah gave Nye a push on the nape of the neck that almost sent him to his knees.

"Get down. Keep out o' sight. That sounds like men talking . . ."

Nye crouched beside the cart.

"Yep, here they come, up over the far ridge," muttered Captain Shebnah.

"How many?"

"Two."

"Does one limp?"

"Aye."

Nye's heart thumped. "That's Pell!"

"Like as not. If I'm any judge, they're follering some tracks in the sand."

Nye looked up wildly at the captain.

"What shall I do? Where can I hide?"

"They're starting down the slope now. Soon as they drop into the holler out of sight, I'll tell ye, and you hop up onto the cart with me." Captain Shebnah climbed up onto the cart and sat down.

Nye could hardly believe his ears, nor his eyes, either. He thought the captain must be losing his wits. Did he have it in mind for them to escape by galumphing off in an oxcart? Nye had not seen Belshazzar in action, it was true, but he could not imagine the huge, ponderous beast moving fast enough to outdistance even a man with a limp. Should he hide in back? No, Pell might think to take a look under the canvas. But still, it seemed to be the only chance.

"Now," said Captain Shebnah. "Look sharp, and in you go."

As he issued this order, the old man stood up and lifted the hinged lid of the box he was sitting on — because the driver's seat was just that, a large box. Brightening, Nye scrambled in and lay down. Captain

Shebnah closed the box quietly. The boards of the lid
creaked as he sat down again.

"Giddap, Belshazzar. Hup!"

Belshazzar stirred himself. The cart began to move.

"Ahoy, there! Wait up!"

In the dusty confines of the box, which smelled not
a little of cod, both salt and fresh, Nye trembled as he
recognized the rough voice that had called out.

"Whoa, Belshazzar. Whoa!"

The cart grated to a stop in sandy ruts.

"Good morning."

"Morning."

"We be looking for a runaway boy."

"Be ye?"

"We been a-following of his tracks. He come this way."

"That so? Well, he ain't called on me. Where did he come from?"

"The Dillingham place."

Captain Shebnah's tone was innocent. "Then you come the wrong way. The Dillinghams live over yonder."

Pell's was impatient. "We know that. The boy made a wide circle and come back this way. They're his footprints, all right. Barefoot, small."

"You speaking of the boy from the wreck as was found by John Dillingham?"

"The same."

"Why'd he run off?"

"Nobody knows. Must be off his head from being in the wreck. But I'm responsible for the lad to his uncle and his pa, so I've got to find him."

Three feet from Pell, Nye was holding on to his nose for dear life. It was not the smell of cod, ripe as it was, that was making him do it. It was the dust. The dust was trying every mean trick it could do to tickle and tease a sneeze out of him. Would they never stop talking out there and go away?

"Well, if he come this direction, he must have kept on going," the captain declared. "Leastways, I haven't seen him. Fool young 'uns — more trouble than they're worth. If he was mine, I'd make him dance when I found him! Giddap, Belshazzar. Hup!"

Once again the oxcart began to move, harness clanking, wheels squealing, and this time it kept going. Tears in his eyes, torture in his nose, Nye suffered to the limits of his endurance, and then —

"Ker*choo!*"

The explosion all but blew Captain Shebnah off the box. Nye had held it in as long as he could.

"Hi! Good thing you kept that by you till now," the captain muttered in a low voice. "I'd best blow my nose, in case they heard that," he added, and did so, resoundingly.

Nye seized his nose again, furious at it. Had his sneeze spoiled everything? But the cart continued to jolt along, and the dreaded voice of Pell was heard no more. Before long Captain Shebnah spoke again, still in a low voice, but with less restraint.

"You all right in there?"

"Y-yes, s-sir," replied Nye, not because his teeth

were chattering, but because the words were being jolted out of him.

"Tight quarters, but you'd best stay below for the time being. We're still in a narrow channel, with uncharted rocks ahead, I'm afeerd, because I went and did a fool thing. Let me see, now. It'll take 'em maybe two or three minutes of looking around the place and poking their noses into the shed, which they're doing right now. Then they'll take off down the road after us, and even with that limp your man Pell will be able to overhaul us. I'd say we've got less'n five minutes, all told . . ."

"Wh-what do you m-mean, Cap'n?" cried Nye so sharply that his voice bounced all around him in the box and hurt his ears. "What f-fool thing did you d-do?"

"I set that letter o' yourn down and left it there in the shed, and they'll find it. Pell may know your uncle gave you that dummy letter. If he's smart enough to take a good squint at it, and makes out the name of Cap'n John Gorham on it, then he'll also be smart enough to suspect I'm not traveling alone."

Nye filled the box with a hollow groan at the thought of the letter lying there in the shed.

"Oh, golly! Then let me out, Cap'n, and I'll —"

"Now, hold on! I'll let you out soon enough, just a

few rods farther on, where the road takes a dip out o'
sight. There's a ridge beside the road there. Slip over
the top of it and stay behind it."

Nye felt the cart tip forward down a slope, and then
slow down.

"Whoa, Belshazzar. Whoa!"

Captain Shebnah stood up and lifted the lid of the
box.

"Now jump into that clump of poverty grass, so's
your footprints won't show in the sand, and get t'other
side o' the ridge, where you can hear me but won't be
seen if those fellers come along behind us."

Nye leaped like a cricket. He landed in the bristling
grass on the low ridge beside the road, ran down the
sharp slope on the far side, and turned around. He
could no longer see the captain or the oxcart.

"You all right?"

"Yes, Cap'n!"

"Now keep down, and walk along so's you can hear
me while I keep a-going. Giddap, Belshazzar. Hup!"

Nye could hear the cart begin to move. Crouching
low, he kept pace with it, and listened as Captain
Shebnah gave him instructions in a low voice.

"You see a housetop off to the north'ard?"

"Yes, sir."

"Make straight fer that housetop till you strike the

path. Then turn left and stay on it. It'll bring you to Pamet Harbor. Look for Jabez Snow and his hooker *Spry*. She's not the smartest craft as ever danced across the bay, but with a fair wind such as she's likely to have this morning, she'll make it in good time. Tell Jabez I said he was to take you across with him. With luck, they won't have heard anything as yet down there about you and them fellers as was looking fer you last night. He'll want fifty cents to take you, Jabez will, being Jabez Snow. Give it to him."

"Yes, sir."

"Now, when you get to Plymouth, go straight to the stagecoach office and tell them you want to take the coach to Fall River, and can pay fer your passage. And when you get to Fall River —"

A distant shout interrupted the captain. His next words came in a low growl.

"Here they come, just as I figgered they would. Skedaddle, lad, and good luck!"

For Nye, it was almost the worst moment yet. To give up the comforting company of this kind old man and be on his own again made a huge, aching lump spring into his throat.

"Thank you, Cap'n!" he called in a low, choked voice, and turned toward the housetop that was to be his bearing.

"Ahoy, there! Lay to, blast you!" Pell's shout became words Nye could make out.

"Whoa, Belshazzar. Whoa!" Nye heard Captain Shebnah order in a calm, unhurried way. Crouching, and setting his jaw to stop the trembling of his lips, Nye raced away, watching for the path to the harbor.

Eleven

THE PATH seemed to twist on and on forever across the bleak, desolate moors, curving around the sides of barren slopes, skirting deep pits scooped out in the sand thousands upon thousands of years ago when the Ice Age glaciers melted. The sky was still dull and gray. The early-morning chill lingered in the air. As he hurried along, Nye gulped down the bread with a ravenous appetite.

For a long time he scarcely saw a house, except at a distance. Was he headed in the proper direction? Upon reaching the path, he had turned left as directed; but even so, he felt the gnawing uncertainty that always goes with following a strange path to an unknown place.

When a house appeared close by around a sudden bend, he did not know whether to be sorry or glad, frightened or reassured. A woman picking up an armload of stove wood at a woodpile saw him coming be-

fore he had a chance to pull back. He kept coming at a
steady pace and did his best to look innocent.

The woman's drab poke bonnet and long, faded
dress showed signs of hard wear. She straightened up
to stare at him with the curiosity of a person who sees
few strangers.

"Good morning, ma'am."

"Who are you, boy?"

"I'm from the wreck, ma'am."

What if she had heard about the men who were looking for a boy, and said something about it? He would not know what to reply. She would guess at once that he was the one.

But she did not speak about it. Instead she said, "You're a Britisher, aren't you? I can tell by the way you talk." She said it proudly, as if this were quite an accomplishment on her part.

"Yes, ma'am."

"What were you doing on an American vessel, then?"

"Why . . ." Nye almost gave himself away. But just when he was sure he could think of nothing to reply, he heard himself offering an explanation. The words seemed to blurt out of him of their own accord. "I was the cabin boy, ma'am."

"The cabin boy!"

"I left my ship in Boston and came aboard the *Plympton Belle* there, ma'am. I thought I'd like American ships better."

The woman stared at him and then laughed in a dry way.

"Well, you didn't make much of a pick for your first one, did you?"

"No, ma'am!" Nye managed a feeble grin, and then pointed along the path. "Is this the way to Pamet Harbor, ma'am?"

She nodded. "Less than a mile. Bear left at the fork about a quarter of a mile from here."

"Thank you!"

Nye waved and hurried on, leaving her staring after him. Had she believed him? Would she go tell a neighbor about him, one who might have heard about the incident at the Dillinghams'? Nye ran on harder than ever.

Though it was still very early in the morning, most people in the village were astir, but not many were abroad as yet. Nye caught glimpses of persons in the houses that lined the lane which the path had led him to, but he met no one, for which he was glad. At the end of the lane he could see a wharf and the masts of several small boats, and beyond these an expanse of undivided gray that was both sky and water.

When he reached the end of the lane where it gave onto the wharves, he could see the bow of a small sloop with the name *Abbie D*. A man driving a wagon had stopped to gossip with a man painting a skiff set upside down on four kegs, and they were having an interesting conversation.

"Been over to the beach, Nat?"

"Nope. You?"

"Went yestiddy."

"Pick up anything?"

"Few things. Small vessel, she was."

"So I heard. Two men lost, they say."

"Aye, two."

"Lucky 'tweren't more."

"Aye. One boy run off."

"Run off?"

"Aye. Fellers from the vessel was a-looking for him last night. Boston cap'n's son, they say, going to New York City to join his pa's ship."

"What did he run off for?"

"Don't rightly know. They think he must be out of his head because of the wreck."

"Hmm. Mighty strange."

"Aye. Well, got to get along or Jabez will sail without my barrel of oysters for my Uncle Ned over Plymouth way. He's mighty partial to Wellfleet oysters, is Uncle Ned. G'day, Nat."

"G'day, Ed."

Nye's heart had already been beating fast as he heard himself talked about. It skipped a beat at the mention of "Jabez." The man on the wagon could only mean Jabez Snow. And he was heading straight for him.

Drawing back to keep out of sight, Nye felt so weak

he had to lean against the rough shingles of the cottage he was standing beside. What was he to do now? Maybe Ed would not tell Jabcz Snow about the runaway boy, but the chances were good he would. And even if he didn't, he would probably stay around talking till the *Spry* sailed. The instant Nye put in an appearance, Ed would spot him as the runaway . . .

Or would he?

A thought pulled Nye back from the brink of despair. He found himself remembering the woman with the stove wood saying, "You're a Britisher, aren't you? I can tell by the way you talk." And Tom Dillingham had remarked, "Thee's English? Thee talks different, too."

People would not expect a Boston captain's son to sound like a Britisher!

For once he was glad he talked differently. With his accent as an unexpected weapon, Nye saw his way to a plan of action.

Whistling a tune he hoped sounded merry, he swaggered around the corner with his hands in his pockets and made straight for Nat, the man who was painting the skiff.

"Good morning, sir!"

Nat glanced up from his work, and his paintbrush stopped in mid-air. His eyes were immediately suspicious. But before he could say anything, Nye asked a question.

"Haven't seen anything of a tyke about my size, only younger and a Yankee, have you, sir?"

In the back of his mind, Nye was recalling the way some of his schoolmates had talked, back in England. Archie Gresham, now. Nye added a touch of Archie to his delivery, to make it even more British. Listening to him, Nat obviously came to the conclusions Nye had hoped he would. First off, this boy was plainly a blasted Limey, and second, he didn't give any indication of being off his head.

"Who are you, young feller?"

"I was cabin boy on the *Plympton Belle*, that was wrecked night before last."

Nat spat over the side of the wharf in a disgusted way.

"What's a Limey like you doing on board an American vessel?"

"I didn't like my old ship — captain was a Tartar. I didn't like the *Plympton Belle* much, either, when she ran ashore first night out, but the boy we're looking for had it worse — he went overboard and was washed ashore."

"Hmm. Well, he ain't been this way that I know of."

"Righto, sir. I was told to ask about him on my way,

and I've done it, but he's not my worry — I've got an errand to do. Can you tell me the way to the *Spry*, sir?"

"What do you want with her?"

"She's going to Plymouth, isn't she?"

While Nat eyed him hard, Nye held his breath. He was afraid the man was going to ask why he wanted to go to Plymouth, and he had suddenly realized he had no reason ready. But then a bluebottle fly came buzzing around Nat's paint can and fell in, and Nat swore at it. He pointed impatiently along the wharf without looking up as he picked the fly out.

"See that wagon yonder?"

"Aye, sir."

"Foller it."

"Thank you, sir!"

Leaving Nat to stamp on the fly, Nye ran off after the wagon. He must be better prepared before he tackled Ed and Jabez Snow. *Why* did he want to go to Plymouth? Why would the cabin boy of a wrecked ship be going to Plymouth?

The wagon had no more than pulled up beside the *Spry*, and the men were still exchanging greetings, when Nye came along. They turned to glance at him.

"Good morning, gentlemen. Could you tell me where I'll find Mr. Jabez Snow?"

Nye put quite a lot of Archie into it this time. He was now as British as John Bull. The man on the boat, a small, bird-like man with spiky hair that crested like a blue jay's topknot, looked him over with a darting glance.

"I'm Snow."

From the wagon Ed was eying Nye with suspicious interest. Nye told the same story he had told Nat, and answered the same questions, except that he said nothing about a missing boy. Then he added, "I'm to go to Plymouth for one of our men to fetch him some things from home. One of our men that was hurt. Captain Shebnah Berry said you were going and would take me."

Jabez Snow's mouth pinched together into a tart smile, and his glance darted to Ed and back again.

"Cap'n Shebnah said so, did he? Well, now, I might and I might not."

Nye remembered what the captain had said about Snow.

"I can pay, sir. The man gave me money."

"Peculiar," observed Ed, who had been staring at him narrowly. "Mighty peculiar. Just this morning I heard tell there's a boy missing from that vessel."

"That's right, sir," said Nye, his heart pounding. He tried to sound more like Archie Gresham than ever.

"A young Yank from Boston, a passenger, he was. He ran off, and we haven't found him yet. Poor little blighter must be off his chump. He went overboard in the storm, so it's a blooming wonder he made it ashore at all."

Ed's suspicions seemed to be subsiding under repeated impacts of Nye's English accent. As for Jabez Snow, the mention of money made him lose interest in minor matters. With eyes as hard and greedy as a jay's, he said, "Cost you fifty cents."

"All right, sir."

Jabez coughed happily. "Well, then, I suppose I can take you. Have to see the color o' your money first, though."

Nye dug out the old leather purse Captain Shebnah had given him, and opened it for the first time. Inside it were one silver dollar and two half-dollars. Nye produced a half-dollar and handed it over as Jabez hopped onto the dock. The small man grasped it as though about to bite it to make sure it was good. He examined the coin on both sides, then thrust it in his pocket.

"Be sailing soon as I put this barrel aboard, and soon as that fool boy that's helping me shows up. You must know your way round a deck, hey?"

"Aye, sir."

"Enough to handle lines when you're told to?"

"Aye, sir." Anything, to get to Plymouth!

"Then we'll go without that lad if he don't show up mighty shortly," said Jabez with sour pleasure. He turned to Ed, who was lifting a small barrel out of the back of his wagon. Nye could hear the grate of oyster shells inside. "I been taking that Quaker lad o' Dillingham's along to learn the ropes."

"And paying him next to nothing, if I know you," said Ed with a broad wink.

"I'm learning him now, ain't I?" squawked Jabez, looking as though he had had his feathers ruffled. "Why should I have to pay him a fortune when I'm learning him seamanship?"

"You're a regular philanthropist, Jabez, that's what you are," declared Ed, with a guffaw. "Here, get my oysters belowdecks, and keep them cool."

Fortunately, neither of the men had noticed the horrified look Nye's face had taken on. Behind them, footsteps pattered onto the wharf, and Jabez Snow, looking around, said crossly, "Well, here he comes, and about time, too!"

Twelve

THE IMPORTANT THING was to speak first. It was his only chance. Smiling as best he could, Nye said, "Hello! I'm Archie Gresham. Are you Tom Dillingham? Wasn't that Gorham tyke at your house before he ran off?"

Luckily, Tom Dillingham was so surprised that he stumbled over a loose board in the wharf and nearly rolled off into the harbor. And by the time he scrambled to his feet, he had his wits about him.

"Hello. Yes, he was there."

"That's what Mr. Pell said."

"Oh." Tom stared at Nye with a wooden face. Meanwhile Jabez Snow had been shaking his head and chirping disgustedly.

"Always falling over his own feet — same way on the boat — be a wonder if I ever make a sailor out of him! Let's see if you two stout lads can carry this here barrel aboard," added Jabez, never one to work if he could find willing hands elsewhere. "Time we was under way!"

The *Spry* was a small and none too graceful sloop, blunt in the bow and broad in the beam. Nye hoped Captain Shebnah was right about their having a fair wind. Without it, he could not imagine the *Spry* going anywhere at more than a snail's pace. Of all names, *Spry* was one she seemed least likely to live up to.

While Jabez Snow, assisted by Tom, got her under way, Nye stayed clear and watched. He noticed that Tom took orders smartly and acquitted himself well as Jabez's crew, and was not as awkward as Jabez pretended. From time to time Nye gazed back at the village they were leaving. He could see Ed's wagon moving off slowly along the waterfront. He could see Nat at work on his skiff, and probably still swearing about that fly that had caused him trouble. And Nye could see a man on horseback appear from one of the lanes.

With sudden concern Nye leaned forward at the rail to peer across the gray waters of the harbor, back at the wharves. Somehow the figure on the horse suggested Pell. Even as he strained his eyes to make sure, however, the *Spry* picked up a breeze at the harbor mouth and began to lumber ahead with more assurance, and the dull light turned the distant figure into a mere stick on horseback.

Could it be Pell? If it was, and he happened to ask questions of the right person — of Nat, painting his skiff, or of Ed, stopping his wagon somewhere to gossip with a crony . . . Still, what could Pell do now? And the whole thing was probably just imagination, anyway. Hoping for the best, Nye turned his attention to watching for a chance to talk to Tom.

Once they were well into open water, with their course set and the wind holding steady, the chance came. With Jabez aft at the tiller, the boys were able to stand in the bow and hold a low-voiced conversation without being overheard.

First Nye told Tom about his adventures since leaving Tom's house. Then he explained his reason for running away.

"So that's it!" said Tom. "Well, Ma didn't cotton to that man's looks at all, from the minute he walked in."

"Your ma helped me a lot when she told them the wrong place for where the tunnel came out."

"Ma hated to tell a lie, but she said that was one time when it would have been a worse sin to tell the truth."

"I had to tell a lie about who I was, to get on board

here — but I'd do worse than that to help save my pa."

"And I'd not blame thee." Tom chuckled as he remembered something else. "My pa was pleased as Punch to know someone had gotten use out of his tunnel!"

Jabez Snow called Tom away to trim the jib, and for a while Nye was alone at the rail, looking out over rippling water toward a horizon that was becoming more and more distinct as the day improved. In the eastern sky a fuzzy glow with a pale yellow disk in the center showed where the sun was trying to break through and burn off the haze. The *Spry* plowed placidly ahead, but the peaceful mood of the moment did not last long for Nye. Because after a while Jabez glanced back and said, "Now, who's that clearing the harbor, and where's he bound for, I wonder?"

Tom applied his keener young eyes to the question.

"Looks like the *Abbie D.*, sir."

"So she does, so she does. I was just about to say so. Well, now, what's Nat up to? Didn't think he was going anywheres today."

The *Abbie D.!* Had somebody hired her for a special trip? And had Nat told that somebody about the British cabin boy who came along looking for the

Spry — somebody who would know the *Plympton Belle* had not had any such cabin boy? With these uneasy questions plaguing him, Nye stared back at the speck on the water behind them, hoping to see her turn and head away in another direction. But the speck came steadily on.

When he could, Nye told Tom about the man he had seen appear on horseback.

"I hope it's not him. Can we stay ahead of the *Abbie D.?*"

"I think so, but she's likely to gain on us some."

The rest of the four-hour sail was an anxious vigil for Nye. He tried not to act too interested in the other boat, so as not to make Jabez Snow wonder about him, because Jabez was doing enough wondering already about the *Abbie D.*

"What in Tophet could be bringing Nat this way?" he muttered aloud in a fretful voice. And slowly, slightly, the distance between them closed. Ahead of the *Spry*, at last, the long low line of the Plymouth shore appeared, but seemed never to draw any closer. Pressing his fist hard on the *Spry*'s rail, Nye begged her under his breath to *move*. But the *Spry* continued to plod on in her ungainly way, and by the time Plymouth finally consented to appear beyond the long bar at the harbor entrance, the *Abbie D.* was not half an hour's sail behind them.

"I'm going to make a run for it as soon as we touch," Nye muttered to Tom.

"Good luck! I wish I could go with thee."

"Tell Cap'n Shebnah what I did."

"I will."

When they reached the dock at Plymouth, Nye was over the side and ashore before Tom had even made a line fast.

"Thank you, sir!"

141

"What's your hurry?" Jabez, holding the *Spry* in at the stern, blinked at him in surprise, but Nye did not stop to reply. He was already running, waving good-by over his shoulder to Tom and receiving a wistful wave in return.

He asked the first person he met where the stage-coach office was, and was directed straight up a nearby street. A moment later he was passing through the swinging doors of an office he had identified by the notices out front. One, which bore an engraving of a Fall River Line steamboat, announced that the stage to Fall River left from that point. The other boasted an equally dashing engraving of a steamboat, and told of a special excursion leaving from New Bedford. Inside at the counter, behind an iron grille, stood a large, pompous man with the air of a transportation overlord who stood at the crossroads of the world.

"When does the stage go to Fall River, please?" Nye asked breathlessly.

The man turned with ceremonious deliberation and consulted a large clock on the wall. It seemed to take him forever to do it.

"In less than an hour's time."

"Not sooner?" cried Nye, and drew a severe look.

"The Fall River stage goes like clockwork, every day same time, and not before."

Crestfallen, Nye turned and trudged outside again. If only Pell were not on the *Abbie D.*, everything would be perfect. But if he was, then Nye hoped wildly for one of two things. Either she would run aground coming into the harbor, or Pell would slip coming off her and break his ugly neck! In broad daylight, on dry land, Nye no longer felt the same fear of the man. Instead, he began to feel angry. And the more he thought about it, the more Nye's spirits began to pick up. After all, everything was not lost, not by a long way. If he could not go to Fall River on the stagecoach, he could get to New York City by some other method and some other route. All he had to do was stay clear of Pell — and the best way to do that was to keep an eye on the man and see what *he* did.

Returning to the waterfront by a roundabout way, beyond the wharves, Nye found himself an ideal observation post from which to watch the *Abbie D.* arrive. A dory had been dragged up into the beach grass well above the high water mark. Sitting on the far side of it, Nye commanded a good view of the wharves while remaining almost invisible himself. From this vantage point he watched the *Abbie D.* round into the harbor and tie up not two boat-lengths from the *Spry*. He groaned when he saw Pell climb onto the dock.

He expected to see Pell walk over to the *Spry* to

talk to Jabez Snow, but instead the man did a surprising thing. He headed as fast as he could go toward the same street Nye himself had been directed to earlier, the street that led to the stagecoach office.

Leaping up, Nye raced back the way he had come. He wanted to find a place from which to keep an eye on the stage office before Pell, limping up the street, could get there. A hundred yards from the office he found a narrow lane where he could peep around the corner of a house and through a hedge with little chance of being noticed. In front of the office the stagecoach had now appeared with a team of big grays harnessed to it. Nye had scarcely taken up his post when Pell turned the corner and, after a sharp look around, entered the office.

A wait ensued that tried Nye's patience. Pell did not reappear. A hostler who had been adjusting the harness finished his job and put his head inside the doors to announce the fact. The coachman appeared and stood beside the coach picking his teeth, having plainly fortified himself for the journey with a good dinner. A middle-aged couple came out and were helped into the coach. Another passenger, an elderly sea captain from the looks of him, joined them, and made a pang go through Nye as he thought of Captain Shebnah.

The coachman turned and called inside, and then began to climb up onto the box. The stagecoach was about to leave. At that moment Pell came limping out of the office and did the last thing Nye expected him to do. He climbed into the coach. The coachman watched him, made sure the door was closed, then settled himself on the box. His whip cracked, the team strained forward, and the coach began to move. It rolled around a corner, and was gone. Pell was gone.

Thirteen

FOR SEVERAL SECONDS Nye was too astonished to move. Then he ran up the street to the next corner and stared after the stagecoach until it rolled out of sight.

Why was Pell going to Fall River? There could be only one reason. He must be going there to take the steamboat to New York City. But why was he doing that? Why had he made no effort to look for Nye?

Whatever the reason, Pell's sudden departure left Nye feeling almost lightheaded. All at once he was no longer being pursued. But on the other hand, how was he going to get to New York City himself, now that he could not go to Fall River? There was still that to be worked out. He turned and looked across the street at the stage office. Had Pell said anything about him to the man in the office? It did not seem likely, because in that case the man would have told Pell that

a bo   g his description had just come into the
office   arlier, and then surely Pell would have
come   him. It should be safe, then, for him
to go in   find out what other way there might
be to ge   ork City. As he stood outside the
office, wo   s courage to go in again, the notices posted   ht his eye. He took a closer look
at the second

Nye stared   ster, spellbound. The magic
words "New-Y   seemed to pulse and glow
before his eyes.   d reach New Bedford by
Wednesday morr.   Then he realized he did not
even know what day it was. He whirled and startled an
old lady half out of her wits by rushing at her as she
was passing by.

"Please, ma'am, what day is this?"

"Land sakes, boy! Don't fly at a body that way!"

"I'm sorry, ma'am, I didn't mean to. But, *please* —"

"I'm blessed if I know what's got into you young
'uns these days!" she grumbled, straightening her bonnet, which she seemed to feel had been knocked awry.
"What is it you wanted to know?"

"What day is it, please?"

"I declare, you talk just like Mr. Pemberton, that
Episcopalian minister, and he's an Englishman. Are
you English?"

AMERICAN PARTY RALLY

The Know-Nothing Party Knows Something
YOU Ought to Know!

The Steamboat
CONCORD

Capt. R. C. Congdon, will leave New Bedford, from the foot of Walburn-st., tomorrow morning,

WEDNESDAY,

October 12, at 7½ o'clock, for the purpose of conveying Delegates to the MASS MEETING, to assemble in New-York City, at 8 o'clock in the evening of the same day — returning Thursday morning.

Fare each way, One Dollar.   **Children half price.**

"Yes, ma'am, part," said Nye, biting his lip as he tried to be patient. "I was wondering what day it is," he reminded her.

"Well, now, if that's not a strange question! It's Tuesday, of course. What day did you think it would be?"

Nye was in luck again. He found a man, a wainwright, who was returning on horseback to New Bedford after repairing wagons in Plymouth. At first the man did not want to be bothered with Nye, but in the end he took him up behind on the horse when Nye offered to pay for the inconvenience.

It was a long, hard ride to New Bedford, thirty-eight miles away. They stopped twice at taverns along the road, and at the second the wainwright, Joshua Huggins, stayed quite a while and drank a good deal of ale. Nye, in a corner of the smoky room filled with local farmers, struggled hard to stay awake as he watched Josh drink up the money he had given him. He was afraid the man might leave him there if he fell asleep. But in the end Josh got to his feet somewhat unsteadily and called gruffly to Nye; they resumed their journey through what was by now a chill, moonlit night.

The rest of the ride was a matter of half-awake, half-asleep misery for Nye, hanging on to Josh's thick waist with his head bobbing this way and that as, time after time, he dropped off to sleep, only to be jolted awake by the horse's next stride.

When at last they reached the livery stable where the wainwright kept his horse, Nye stumbled into an empty stall and spent the rest of the night on its straw. Belshazzar's stall had been more pleasant, but Nye did not care. At first he plunged into a black oblivion of exhaustion, but he was too inwardly excited to sleep long. In the morning he woke early, startled awake by a nightmare in which a giant barrel bounded at him across an immense deck. He bought some rolls in a bakeshop and walked through the streets like a young Ben Franklin, eating them. At 7:30 he was on the steamboat *Concord* on his way to New York City. He was allowed to come on board by a man who laughed at the sight of him, but was glad enough to take his money.

At any other time Nye would have been excited about his first trip on a steamboat. Even now he did quite a bit of gawking at the boat's luxurious furnishings, and quite a bit of marveling at the speed she was making. But he was too anxious about what lay ahead, and too impatient to get there, to really enjoy it all.

The Know-Nothing Party, as the American Party was popularly called even by its members, seemed to Nye

to be a political party of an extremely noisy persuasion. Almost immediately the delegates began to get warmed up for their mass meeting. Some went marching around the deck, four abreast where they could, singing political songs that paid no special compliments to either the Democrats or the Republicans. Others gave impromptu political speeches in corners of the grand saloon or out on the promenade deck. Still others simply got into prolonged and noisy arguments. There were two or three interesting fist fights which proved that party solidarity was not all it might be. One man's stovepipe hat got knocked overboard and went bobbing away behind in the wake, to the great amusement of everybody but its owner.

From a conversation Nye overheard between a delegate and one of the steamboat officers, he learned that the party had once been a secret society. In those days, it seemed, when anybody asked a member any questions about the party, he always said he knew nothing. That was how it had gotten its strange nickname — the Know-Nothing Party.

Nye did little more than peep into the grand saloon and the dining saloon. The grand saloon was a sumptuous, high-ceilinged room with deep carpets underfoot and splendid glass chandeliers overhead, with armchairs upholstered in red plush, and a balcony running around the sides of the room where people could stroll and look down on the scene. The dining saloon was equally magnificent. Nye was very hungry, but he did not dare enter such a place looking as shabby as he did, and barefooted as well. Not that he could have paid the fifty cents that dinner cost there, anyway — his money was almost gone.

He found his way to the galley and asked if he could do something to earn some dinner. He was quickly put to peeling a mountain of potatoes, but he was fed well and he peeled cheerfully. It was something to do, a way to pass the hours that still separated him from the object of his long journey. Indeed, it seemed as if ever since he had climbed out the window at his grandfather's house he had spent endless time waiting to get places. And even now, now that he was almost there, a final problem began to trouble him.

How could he best go about getting aboard the *Ellen?*

If Pell had gone to New York City the night before from Fall River, he was already there by now. By now Uncle Daniel must be there too, and Pell would have told him about the wreck of the *Plympton Belle* and about how he, Nye, had escaped. They would be on the lookout for him. They would surely try to prevent him from reaching his father. He would have to be very careful about approaching the pier where the ship lay.

After he had thought the matter over for several dozen potatoes, a simple plan occurred to him. Instead of going straight to the *Ellen*, he would go to some other ship nearby. He would ask to see the captain. He would explain that he was the son of Captain Gorham of the *Ellen Gorham*, and would tell the captain as much of his story as he had to in order to convince him he needed help. He would ask to have a seaman sent to the *Ellen* urgently requesting that Captain Gorham come see the other captain at once. The seaman would bring his father back with him, and that would be that.

It seemed like a good plan to Nye. At any rate, it was the best he could think of, and he resolved to try it.

"Get out on deck and have a look at a real city!" one of the cooks' helpers had told him. Relieved of his paring knife, Nye left the galley and reached the promenade deck just as the *Concord* cleared a narrow passage called Hell Gate.

"Now it's down the East River, around the Battery at the tip of Manhattan, and then we tie up at Pier Ten on the Hudson River side," he heard one passenger explaining to a less worldly friend.

All during the sweep down the heavily traveled East River, Nye's excitement mounted and mounted until he could hardly keep from throwing his head back and shouting. He was almost there! The desperate journey that had begun so long ago from his bedroom window in England was nearly over at last. To Nye, that final few miles past the New York City waterfront was a splendid confusion of red brick buildings, shipping, towboats, ferries, barges, piers, and slips, all blurred together under a sky still streaked with the pinks and blues and purples of a spectacular sunset, about to deepen into dusk. One great ship after another lay alongside the piers, sailing ships and steamships both, ships with strange and wonderful names, and home ports that called to mind half the countries in the world and all the seven seas.

"There's the Battery, up ahead there," the well-traveled man announced. "Won't be long now!"

Not far ahead, at the tip of the island of Manhattan, Nye could see a round fort. He glanced back at the passing scene of the East River piers just in time to get the thrill of his life. For an instant the stern of a ship alongside the pier they were passing swam before his eyes. Then he read the letters on the nameplate:

ELLEN GORHAM
BOSTON

In the midst of the shouting, singing crowd that lined the rail, Nye's wild shout went unnoticed.

"Pa!" he cried at the top of his lungs. It was all he could do not to slip through the rail and dive overboard. It was excruciating to sweep past the proud ship, to be within yards of his father, and to be unable to do a thing about it. Nothing but watch while the ship and the pier dropped behind. Pier 27! At least the number had burned itself into his mind. He saw a tall man standing at the taffrail of the *Ellen Gorham* as they passed, watching them go by, and just too far away in the fading light of dusk for Nye to be certain — but the man *looked* like his father.

"It could have been!" he told himself, warmed by the very possibility. "It could have been!"

The *Concord* swung around the Battery and nearer her Hudson River pier. As the great walking beam pumped her paddle wheels the last few hundred yards of the journey, Nye hurried to the point forward of the starboard paddle wheel where the gangplank would go ashore. His breath was coming fast, and his heart was beating as if it had its own walking beam hurrying it along. He ducked and wriggled forward through the forest of paunches and legs that separated him from the gangplank. He was going to be first off the boat, or as near to it as he could.

At last, after what seemed like endless fussing and fiddling, the great steamboat lay alongside the pier. The gangplank clattered onto the dock, and Nye, pressing forward, felt as if he were being carried across it by a great and powerful wave. His feet touched shore, and he was weaving ahead through the crowd, running, until he broke through the first rank and was speeding on down the pier ahead of everybody.

It was the worst thing he could have done, of course. It made things so much easier for the man who was waiting.

Fourteen

As NYE REACHED the street at the end of the pier, he felt one of his arms suddenly seized and twisted up painfully behind his back, and fingers touching his windpipe in an almost casual way that made it impossible for him to shout. The man who bundled him toward a waiting hackney carriage was an expert.

"Run away from home, will ye?" said the man in a loud voice which Nye knew was meant for passersby. "Wait'll your pa tends to you, young feller!"

At that moment Nye learned a bitter lesson in the ways of the world. He learned how true it was that clothes make the man, and the boy as well. The street was full of traffic, and of people walking by, but nobody came to his rescue. Nobody protested against the way he was being treated. Shabby and barefooted as he was, he looked like nothing more than a street urchin. And because he did, nobody took his existence seriously. Everybody assumed that if the man who held him had bothered to seize such a ragamuffin of a boy, he must have good and sufficient reasons for doing so.

Another man opened the door of the battered old landau. Nye got only a fleeting glimpse of him as he was shoved past into the carriage, but he knew him at once.

The man holding Nye pushed him inside with a force that sent him flat on his face on the carriage floor. The second man stepped in behind him, sat down, closed the door, and planted his foot cruelly on Nye's ribs before Nye could move.

"Stay where you are and don't open your mouth, or by the Lord Harry I'll kick you senseless! Well, now, Master Nye, it's a pleasure to see you again. A real pleasure, after all the trouble you've put me to." Red-Eye Pell sounded relieved, and much pleased with himself. A whip cracked. The carriage began to move. "You gave me many an anxious minute today, I don't mind saying, after I found the *Ellen Gorham* hadn't sailed as expected."

Nye could not help gasping at that. Pell heard him, and laughed.

"That's right. She was ready to sail on a day's notice, and a messenger come straight here by the fastest way as soon as you were on board the *Plympton Belle*. He told your pa you hadn't come from England on the

Griffin. That was all your pa was waiting for. He would have been gone by now if it hadn't been for some fool coming along with a last-minute consignment of cargo he couldn't resist — as if she wasn't carrying a fortune already! That come nigh to spoiling everything, that did. Here I'd hurried here from Plymouth — oh, I knew you'd come over on the *Spry*, never fear, but I didn't bother running after you any more, because by then I figgered your pa had sailed, anyway. Only he hadn't, of course."

Pell paused for a self-satisfied chuckle.

"But even then, I had you. There was only one way you could have got here in time, and I headed you off from that. I went to Fall River myself. That only left one way for you to come — by way of that special excursion from New Bedford. When I got here, I remembered that — and I was right, wasn't I, boy?" crowed Pell, prodding Nye's ribs with his heavy boot. He was a man who had gone through a great deal of frustration and anxiety. Now that he had finally won the game, he wanted to rub it in thoroughly and enjoy his triumph.

"Now, with the ship supposed to be sailing on a day's notice, all I had to do was to see to it you stayed with the *Plympton Belle* when she touched Nantucket, and make sure she was slow about getting under way again. Then the *Ellen Gorham* would have been sure to

159

go without you, and you'd never have been any the wiser about who had arranged matters that way. You would have blamed me. But then you had a look at that letter you was carrying, and now you know something, don't you? You know something, eh?"

"Yes, I know!" Nye blurted angrily, and realized almost at once that this was exactly what Pell had wanted to hear. The man's exultant laughter, mean-hearted and malevolent, told him so.

"Course you did! He didn't want you ever to know — but things didn't work out that way, did they?" said Pell. For some reason that Nye could not immediately fathom, Pell was delighted that Nye knew.

They had not gone far when the carraige stopped. The weight of a man climbing down from the box made it jounce, and then the carriage door opened.

"Take him inside, Jack," Pell said to the second man, who had the appearance of being a young seaman. "And you march inside without making any fuss, or you'll wish you hadn't."

Nye was hauled out of the carriage onto his feet and hustled inside a house. They were in a side street, ill-lit and deserted. In the glimpse he got of the street, Nye saw no one who might have helped him even if he had tried to call out. Inside, Nye could see nothing, but the air was full of odd and assorted smells that somehow suggested the hold of a ship to him, as though he might be in a warehouse of sorts. In a moment Pell came in and lighted a small candle lantern he was carrying. Nye could see he had been right. In shadowy rooms to his left he could make out the shapes of barrels and bales and boxes.

"Upstairs," ordered Pell. Jack jostled Nye in the direction of a steep flight of stairs that led to a landing two thirds of the way up and then turned to the left. Slowly they mounted the steps. Odds and ends of rubbish gathered in the back corner of the landing beside an empty barrel gave the impression of a halfhearted clean-up effort, but the stairs were still dirty. Only the smooth banister Nye grasped on the way up indicated that the house must have once seen better days. At the top of the stairs a dingy hallway led to a small room at the far end. Judging from the tables and chairs that were the principal part of its shabby furnishings, it was used as an office. Nye was shoved into a chair and told to stay there.

"Now, then, Jack," said Pell. "Go to the ship and tell him we have the boy. And tell him he knows. Mind you speak to him out of earshot of everyone. Ask him what's to be done now."

Jack nodded and left. Pell closed the door behind

him, set the lantern on a table, kicked a chair out for himself, and sat down facing Nye. He tipped his chair back against the door and resumed his enjoyment of the turn of events.

"Aye, you were a slippery one, you were. Of course, the wreck spoiled plans to begin with. For a while, it seemed as if you'd never run out of luck. Slipping out of that house the way you did, and then getting away again with the help of that old fool of a Cap'n What's-his-name — oh, yes, I know he helped you, though he denied it. I should have bashed him one whilst I had the chance. You had me walking my poor feet off there, and me with a game leg to boot.

"By and by I saw I might as well stop wasting time on you, since by then you couldn't get here in time to do any harm anyway — or so I thought. So I hired me a horse and rode down to the harbor. I'd got wind of the fact there was a sloop going to Plymouth, but I was too late to catch her. And you were on her! The hooker I hired wasn't much better, or I might have caught up with you then and there. But then, once I had time to stop and think on the way over, it come over me all of a sudden, and I says to myself, 'Why wear yourself out trying to hunt him down when he can't get there in time now anyway?' Turns out I come near being wrong. But no matter. Catching you here is better than doing it in Plymouth, much better. No fuss, nothing to explain to anyone — much better. All's well that ends well," said Pell in an almost sanctimonious tone of voice, as though Fate had finally bestowed a well-deserved reward on him after treating him badly. "Now all we have to do is sit here and wait to see what story Jack brings back."

Nye had listened to Pell's gloating recital and found the details just as painful as Pell obviously hoped he would. But at the same time his mind was busy with other questions. When was the *Ellen* going to sail? How soon? What could he do? How could he get away from Pell? He betrayed himself by glancing at the lantern on the table. Pell noticed. He tipped his chair forward, rose to his feet, and picked up a thick stick, almost a cudgel, that was standing in one corner, leaning against the wall. He smacked the end of it menacingly against the hard palm of his hand.

"I've orders you're not to be mistreated," he growled, "but just you try to knock over that there lamp, or do anything clever like that, and I'll mistreat you good and proper."

The light in his bleary, bloodshot eyes, glittering with anticipation, made it clear he meant what he said. Nye hung his head and made no reply. Pell sat down again, but laid the stick across his lap. Minutes dragged by. Then Nye could hear the front door being opened and shut downstairs. If Uncle Daniel was on board the *Ellen*, and Jack had already given him the message and returned, then the ship and Pier 27 were not far away. Pell stood up and pulled his chair away from the door. A quick step sounded on the stairs. The door was flung open. Nye gasped.

"Uncle . . . !"

It was he, true enough, but a frighteningly altered Uncle Daniel. He had aged beyond belief. He looked seriously ill. His glowing eyes, sunk deep in their sockets, his hollowed-out cheeks, and his ghastly pallor combined to make a death's-head of his face. Especially

was it so when his lips pulled back from his teeth in a horrible attempt at a smile. A smile!

"Nye! Thank God you're safe!" Without even taking his eyes from his nephew, he gestured impatiently at Pell. "Go downstairs and wait."

"Well, now, sir . . ." Pell seemed to find the order not to his taste, and was about to protest. A single burning glance from Nye's uncle made him think better of it. He left them alone, and his dragging step could soon be heard on the stairs. Uncle Daniel stood in front of Nye, now looking down at him and shaking his head. Suddenly, as suddenly as he had smiled his frightful smile, his thin face twisted in an agony of regret.

"How vile, how vile! Why did it come to this? You need never have known. Curse that wreck, curse the thousand and one mischances that have always been my lot!"

He cocked his head sideways, fixed Nye with bright, staring eyes, and began to speak in measured tones as if he were explaining the most reasonable proposition in the world. The effect of it was to make Nye's skin crawl.

"Well, no matter, no matter, we must make the best of it, Nye. You must understand it is all for the best. You must understand the justice of it. You are rightfully my son, Nye, not his. You should have been mine, just as your mother should have been mine. My only thought for you, once he is out of the way, is to raise you as my own son. I'll give you everything, you'll be my sole heir — everything will go to you in the end! You must see how right this is, Nye. You must see it."

Staring into his uncle's fanatical eyes, Nye came up against a shattering certainty. He knew he was not looking into the eyes of a sane man. Uncle Daniel really believed in what he was saying, and expected Nye to accept it!

"You see, Nye, it was I who loved your mother first, not he, and she would have married me if — if *he* hadn't won her, just as he always won everything else. *I* went to sea first, *I* had command first! But then, because of one mishap that wasn't fully my fault, your grandfather decided I was not cut out for command. He gave the chance to my brother — and of course *he* never made mistakes, *he* swept everything before him. Next it was your mother . . . Oh, he's a strong man, a strong man, but even the strongest have their weak spots, and he has his. The only place I could beat him was on paper, and I've done that for years. Years! But even your unsuspicious fool of a father might find out if matters went much further. The time has come to be rid of him — and then, when he's out of the way, we'll go bring your mother home, and we'll live happily the way we were always meant to."

A deep, numbing chill spread through Nye's body.

"B-but my mother's dead!"

Uncle Daniel drew back angrily.

"Nonsense! You mustn't say things like that. She's not dead. How can you say such a thing? I won't have it!"

Abruptly he smiled his hideous smile again, and his reasonable tone of patient explanation returned. "You'll see. After *he's* out of the way, we'll go and . . . Nye, you *must* see that I'm right about all this," he declared, as though he were admonishing a small child, "because otherwise I don't know what I can do with you. You can see that, can't you?"

What I can do with you! In his uncle's mad gaze Nye saw life and death. Any show of resistance was pointless — instinctively he understood that. Somehow he managed to say, "Yes, Uncle Daniel. I see."

His uncle's face became radiant — and he did a horrible thing. He threw his arms around Nye and hugged him.

Nye's head reeled, but a strange combination of pity and guile made him able to accept the hug and even return it. The thought of his father's danger made him ruthless, carried him through. If there was any chance at all, it could only be preserved by playing a deadly game of Pretend with Uncle Daniel.

"My boy! My boy! I'm so pleased." Uncle Daniel released him and strode to the door. He pulled it open and called in a loud voice.

"Pell!"

"Aye, sir?"

"Come up."

Pell clumped up the stairs.

"Take good care of the boy till I return."

"Aye, sir," said Pell without enthusiasm.

Uncle Daniel stepped outside into the hall. A murmured conversation took place. Enough of it reached Nye's ears to thoroughly alarm him. "An offshore wind . . . If it rises, she sails within the hour . . . He's eager to go . . . A towboat is standing by . . ."

Nye listened with his heart in his mouth, and stared at the candle lantern on the table. Here was his chance. But what good would it do to knock over the lantern and try to make a run for it in the dark, with two grown men in the way? And before Nye could make up his mind to try, Uncle Daniel had stepped into the room again.

"Pell will stay with you here until I return," he said. A sly look of cunning veiled his eyes as if all the things he had said moments before had never been mentioned. This was intended, Nye realized, for Pell's benefit. How much did Pell understand about the true state of his uncle's mind? Uncle Daniel stepped out of the room again, and Nye could hear him leaving. Pell came in and closed the door. His lip curled as he set his chair in front of the door again.

"He's a strange one, your uncle, but he pays well. That's the main thing, he pays well," said Pell complacently. It was plain he had no idea he was dealing with a madman. It was plain that Uncle Daniel was still able to show the world a mask that passed for a sane man's face.

"Puts him in an intersting fix, now that you know about him. What's he to do with you? What *can* he do? How can he ever draw an easy breath again as long as you're around? I'm interested to see how he works it out. Mighty interested!"

Pell's cruel grin helped Nye to understand why he had been so pleased to find that Nye knew about his uncle. Now it was not only his father's life, but his own as well, that hung in the balance. This was what pleased Pell.

The minutes were ticking by, and the snatches of conversation he had overheard seemed to dance in his head like painted demons round a victim tied to a stake. "An offshore wind . . . If it rises, she sails within the hour . . . He's eager to go . . . A towboat is standing by . . ." As hard as he could, Nye tried to think of some way to escape. But with Pell planted against the door, watching him carefully, it seemed hopeless. He needed something to fight with, but he had no weapon.

Something, perhaps the branch of a tree, tapped against the dingy window behind Nye, part of some tree struggling for life in a narrow courtyard. Pell listened, and leered at him.

"Wind," he said. "Wind coming up. Your pa will like that."

Wind! Nye could have shrieked at the thought of it. A lethal wind ready to blow his father to certain death. All sorts of wild images tumbled through Nye's mind, like a bad dream. Then one of them came again, and again, persistently. Something flickered at the back of his mind. Nye thought and thought. And then, after a while, he began to cry.

Fifteen

IT WAS NOT HARD to let himself go. He had never felt more forlorn and alone in the world, more lost. It was easy enough to cry. He did a thorough job of it.

At first Pell enjoyed the spectacle, this evidence of complete despair and surrender. But after a while he grew bored with the sound of it.

"Ah, stop your blubbering, before I give you something to blubber about," he ordered with lazy contempt. Nye raised his arm as though to ward off a blow, and cowered in his chair.

"You leave me alone!" he sobbed. "My Uncle Daniel said you had to treat me well!"

"I heard what he said, but avast blubbering all the same. You sound like a blooming baby, squalling away."

It was not easy to stop, once he had started. And Nye purposely took his time about stopping. But then a sound rasped his nerves again. Tap . . . tap . . . tap

. . . Again, like a message of doom, the branches tapped the window as the wind stirred them. Time was running out. Nye dragged his sleeve across his face and sniveled as wretchedly as though the last vestiges of any spirit had left him. For a time he sat with a hangdog air, gulping and sobbing. Then he looked up at Pell with bleary eyes, and whined out a request.

"What?" Pell was annoyed. "Never mind that. You just sit there and —"

"I can't!" whined Nye. "Please, Mr. Pell, I'm going to be sick if I don't go . . ."

It was the sort of problem that could only be solved one way, and that was by a trip downstairs to a back room. Pell stood up threateningly.

"All right, but give me any trouble and I'll make you smart for it!" But it was obvious he was no longer worried about a boy who had reached his breaking point and had become such a limp, sodden, spineless baby as Nye. Gathering Nye's collar in one hand, he pulled the door open with the other, picked up the candle lantern, and yanked Nye into the hall.

"Pick up your blasted feet!" he ordered as Nye shuffled forward like a rag doll. Down the stairs they went, and through the storeroom to a cubbyhole in the back. "Now be quick about it!" Pell shoved him inside and slammed the door on him.

Nye took off his jacket and waited, letting his eyes adjust to the darkness. He waited until Pell roughly demanded to know how long it was going to take him. Nye said he would be out directly.

He was. He wadded up his jacket. He took a deep breath. He said a brief prayer. And he shoved the door open as hard as he could.

At the same instant he slammed the jacket in Pell's face. The candle lantern flew out of the startled man's hand and crashed to the floor. In the sudden blackness Nye darted past him and ran for the front of the building. Shouting murderous threats, Pell fumbled his way after him.

"You varmint, I'll kill you! Don't think you can get away! I'll break every bone in your rotten carcass!"

Pell was too close behind for Nye to try to swing open the heavy front door and slip out. But that had never been his plan anyway. He ran for the stairs and up them as fast as he could. And Pell, surprised by this maneuver, but carried along by his blind rage at having been tricked, followed as rapidly as his game leg would allow.

Gasping as he leaped up the stairs, Nye raced for the landing. Even at that moment the same image filled his mind, the image that had come into it moments before. Just as it had tumbled nightmarishly

173

through his dreams, just as he had imagined it again in the room upstairs, so did the barrel on the *Plympton Belle* come bounding through his mind now, straight toward him. Reaching the empty barrel on the landing, he tugged it over on its side, swung it round toward the stairs, and shoved with all his might.

Pell was halfway up. He heard, more than saw, what Nye was doing.

"Stop that, you —!"

He made one awkward effort to turn back, but it was too late. The barrel, bounding down the steps like a live creature, caught him in the shoulder and sent him tumbling heels over head. It crashed into the wall at the foot of the stairs and caromed off down the hallway. Pell crashed into the wall, and groaned once.

And almost before the barrel had bounded away, Nye was making a flying descent. Life in his grandfather's house had made him an expert at sliding down banisters. He reached the door in a twinkling and dragged it open. Slipping outside into the street, he pulled the door shut, and ran.

"Pier Twenty-seven! Please, sir, where's Pier Twenty-seven?"

"Foot of the street and bear right."

"Thank you!"

There was a market, with open stalls on both sides of the street, with smoky lanterns throwing bright light over the black cobblestones, and there were crowds of people strolling through, and stopping to bargain, and there were horses and wagons, but all was a blur to Nye, a blurred scene through which he ran with only one thing in mind — to reach the ship.

At last there were docks, and bowsprits of great sailing ships thrust proudly over the waterfront street. He wheeled around the corner to the right. There was no time for anything now but to go straight to the ship. He had to hope that Uncle Daniel and the mate and the seaman called Jack would all think he was safe in the warehouse with Pell. No one would be on guard. And yet, if one of them happened to see him coming . . . !

Up ahead he could see a great ship with her deck bright with flaring lanterns. A ship astir with the last-minute bustle of departure. It was then that Nye made one of the most important decisions of his life.

It was almost the hardest thing he had ever done — to stop running at such a time — but that was what he decided he must do.

He forced himself to slow down and walk. *Walking,* he suddenly realized, was his best and only disguise.

Running might attract attention, but who would notice a ragamuffin sauntering along the pier? Who would expect him, if he appeared at all, to simply come walking along? Resolutely, Nye thrust his hands into his pockets and began to saunter.

It was an agonizing ordeal. He ground his teeth together to keep them from chattering. He had never been more frightened in his life. He felt as if every eye on the ship were boring into him. To keep from panicking, he tried to tell himself that nobody was looking at him. But was it true? Jack, now. What if Jack was working on deck, and stopped to glance over the rail . . . ?

But meanwile, each tingling step brought the gangplank nearer. He started violently as a seaman came springing down it onto the dock. But the man turned and hurried off in the other direction, toward the stern. Nye's legs had all but given way with fright. Three thousand miles he had come, but those last hundred steps were the longest part of the entire desperate journey. His head swam, and he was suddenly filled with the dreadful conviction that he was going to die, that he was going to drop down dead before he could make the last few steps.

The gangplank was ten feet away, and nobody had cried out. Nobody had rushed down it to intercept him. The distance closed. He set his stumbling feet on the limber boards. Straight ahead of him, two men appeared, the nearer one turning to shake hands with the taller man. A bright lantern hanging from a mast behind them framed the tall man in light and sent golden rays shooting away from him in all directions. Nye's heart filled with joy and pain, with triumph and sorrow. He stopped in his tracks in the middle of the gangplank.

"Pa!" he shouted, his voice breaking. "Pa, it's Nye!"

The smaller man whirled as though he had been shot. He stared at Nye with a face that had gone dead-white. Then his eyes rolled up and he fell to the deck. The tall hat in Uncle Daniel's hand rolled away, righted itself with a pathetic waggle, and settled on the deck, upside down.

"Nye!" cried Captain Gorham, trying to believe his eyes. "What on earth —"

Nye rushed forward and threw himself into his father's arms.

"Pa! It *is* me, it *is!*"

"Bless you, son, it is indeed!" said his father, holding him in a bear-hug that took the breath out of him. "But how — Mr. Larkins! Mr. Larkins, will you look to Mr. Daniel, he's had a shock. Have him carried to my —"

178

"Here, you two, pick him up! I'll run for a doctor myself, sir —"

Nye startled his father by struggling loose.

"Wait! He's one of them! Stop him!"

But Mr. Larkins was already across the gangplank, and Captain Gorham had the further astonishment of seeing his new first mate running off as if the devil himself were after him. And before he had recovered from that surprise, a young seaman sprang to the rail forward and leaped from there to the dock, and also disappeared as fast as he could.

"What in blazes *is* this all about?" cried the baffled captain, who had never seen anything like it in all his years at sea, as he often remarked later on. "And how in blazes did you get here, Nye, when your uncle said you hadn't come at all?"

"Pa, they meant to kill you!"

Captain Gorham stared into his son's face, and then his own expression changed. Painfully, even before Nye could tell his story, his father began to put two and two together into some glimmering of the truth. He stared down at the limp form two seamen were lifting from the deck.

"Good God! He lied to me. Dan lied to me about you, when he said Mr. Willet had not brought you back. I've had an uneasy feeling something wrong was

179

going on, and I've been worried about how ill he looks, but I never dreamed . . . May the Lord deliver us! Come along, son, and let's hear the whole story!"

When the *Ellen Gorham* finally sailed, the sailing was a solemn one. Uncle Daniel was in a sanitarium where he would have the best of care, because it was plain he would never be well again in mind or body. Mr. Larkins and Jack were still at large, dodging the law, and even Pell had managed to disappear before men went to the warehouse to look for him. The shadow of what might have been still hung over the ship. It would take a few days of clean sea breezes to blow it away.

On the happier side, letters had been sent to Captain Shebnah Berry and the Dillinghams, and the captain's money had been scrupulously repaid.

As for the office in Boston, Captain Gorham had arranged to have Uncle Daniel's work carried on by the very man, Mr. Marshall, whom Nye had met when he arrived on the *Griffin*, the man who had walked back to the office with Uncle Daniel and him. And if all went well, perhaps Nye's father and Mr. Marshall would become partners.

"I'm not cut out to stay ashore and go into drydock in any office," growled Captain Gorham. "Not yet, at any rate. Our captains know Amos Marshall, and they'll have confidence in his judgment, the same as I have — he's a fine man with a good head for business. He'll keep us on an even keel, I'm sure of that."

This left only Nye's schooling to be arranged for, and here his father had a surprise for him in the form of a young man who reminded Nye a great deal of his schoolmaster Mr. Snodgrass, except that this young man had a more pleasant expression. They were at sea before Nye's father got around to springing his surprise, and even then he had to wait a day or two, until the young man got over being seasick. When he finally appeared on deck, pale but resolute, Captain Gorham introduced him.

"This is Mr. Townsend, Nye. Mr. Townsend is a graduate of Harvard College, and he's come with us to be your tutor. Maybe your grandpa was right — I might not have time to do a proper job of it myself, and I don't want the old gentleman able to say you're not getting an education every bit as good as that sound British schooling he talked so much about. So Mr. Townsend will tend to making you a scholar, and I'll tend to making you a seaman."

"Yes, Pa!"

It was that last part that Nye liked the sound of best. Glancing at young Mr. Townsend, he was relieved to see an understanding twinkle in his eyes that boded well for the future. Sails cracked overhead, and they all looked up to watch the topsails fill with a freshening breeze. Ahead lay the Horn, the Pacific, and the China Seas. As far as Nye was concerned, life was really beginning at last.